CHRISTINE DORÉ MILLER

Evernight Teen ®

www.evernightteen.com

Copyright© 2021

ISBN: 978-0-3695-0358-9

Cover Artist: Jay Aheer

Editor: Jessica Ruth

CHRISTINE DORÉ MILLER

DEDICATION

For the storm chasers.

CHRISTINE DORÉ MILLER

AWAKENED ARE THE STARRY-EYED

Christine Doré Miller

CHRISTINE DORÉ MILLER

 AWAKENED ARE THE STARRY-EYED

The Starry-Eyed Series, 2

Christine Doré Miller

Copyright © 2021

⊷•◆•⊶

Chapter One

"Congratulations, Oakwood High seniors!" The principal's voice boomed from the crackling speaker atop the worn turf of the school football field.

The crowd erupted in cheers and excited exclamations as the other graduating students leaped to their feet, their polyester caps and gowns gleaming in the harsh sunlight. I slowly stood up, too, my pulse quickening amongst the noise. I dug my fingernails into my soft palms, feeling the chipped black nail polish flake against my skin.

Purple gown. Green grass. White shoes, I said to myself between breaths, focusing only on these few items in my peripheral to keep from drowning in the depths of the past or slipping into the threatening disquiet of the future. My pulse started to stabilize, and I loosened the tension from my fists. *Purple gown. Green grass.*

White shoes. Stephanie is next to me. The sun is out. And I am safe.

"We did it!" Stephanie shouted. The gold tassel from her cap brushed against my face as she came in for a quick, tight hug. She continued chattering, but it was hard to hear over the exuberant buzz that engulfed us. I looked toward the bleachers and scanned the rows of seats until I settled on familiar faces. My mom and dad were waving eagerly, trying to catch my attention, and right next to them was Carter, who flashed a thumbs-up and that signature half-smile that still made me flutter even after a year of dating. My mom pointed toward the parking lot, signaling me to meet them there. I nodded and turned back to Stephanie.

"Andrea, hello? Did you hear me?" she asked.

"Yes, sorry. I know, I can't believe it, either. High school is … over."

"Well, yeah, but that's not what I was saying. I swear, sometimes you're in a different world." Stephanie turned around to see what I had been looking at. "Ohhhhh, never mind, how could I possibly compete with *the* Carter Wells?" She rolled her bright green eyes and tilted her head.

"Shut up," I said playfully. "I'm sorry. I'm listening now."

"I was just saying that I can't believe you're leaving me! We better make this the best summer ever!" she yelled over the noisy crowd.

"I'm not *leaving you*, Steph. I'm going to college! And so are you!"

"Yeah, but my school's barely twenty minutes away. You're going to Chicago!" She turned down her glossy pink lips into an exaggerated pout.

"Yes, and you can visit me in the big fancy city whenever you want," I said, flipping my hair and turning up my nose in an inflated fashion that made us both laugh.

"Yeah, right." She let out a subdued giggle. "As if there'll be room for me in you and Carter's love nest."

"Oh, come on, Steph," I said tensely, feeling the annoyance start to bubble up as I tried to quickly prepare the defense I'd practiced. But before I could retort, I felt a long, lanky arm flop onto my shoulder.

"Ladies, it's official. We are *done* with high school," Ethan exclaimed, pulling me in for a familiar side hug.

Ethan Marks and Stephanie Lang were my closest friends, though they couldn't have been more different. Ethan was humorously tall with a mess of curly blond hair and whimsical sky-blue eyes that were usually full of mischief and laughter. We met in band class during junior high, which was fitting since Ethan was obsessed with all things music. Every spare moment he had was devoted to practicing the worn-out drum set in his garage. School was usually his last priority, so it wasn't surprising to see him so relieved that it was ending.

Stephanie, on the other hand, was my childhood best friend who had never stepped foot in our school's band room. She was in choir and theater and focused sharply on her studies. She excelled in French and literature, which she planned to continue at the local community college this fall. She was petite and energetic, with long, thick auburn hair that was usually straightened from its natural wavy state, and she had light freckles sprinkled across her heart-shaped face. Her carefree boho style was typically complemented with flowing skirts and trendy scarves, and she was quick with advice, jokes, and unapologetic honesty. For years I was the only thing that Stephanie and Ethan had in common, but they had recently grown on each other, which I felt proudly responsible for.

"Good riddance, Oakwood," I replied.

"Andie, we'll talk more later," Stephanie said. "I need to see a few other people before they leave. See you at Jeff's party tonight, right? And you, too, Ethan?"

"You know it!" Ethan exclaimed, giving Stephanie a high five, which she had to get on her tiptoes to reciprocate. I nodded and smiled, even though I hadn't decided if I was going yet. I didn't know if I was ready.

"You heading out?" Ethan asked, his arm still slung around my shoulders.

"Yeah, I guess so," I replied. We started walking toward the parking lot, the surrounding noise getting fainter with every step.

"Hey," I started. "Do you think … I mean, I know today is Oakwood's graduation, but do you think … does, like, *every* school graduate today?"

Ethan sighed. "River Academy graduated last weekend if that's what you're asking."

"That's *not* why I asked," I lied through shaky breaths as the dread hit my stomach and started creeping up my body. *Purple gown. Green grass. White shoes.*

"It's okay, Andie," Ethan said softly. "He's not back in town yet. He's not even in the country. Josh's parents took him on some European vacation for his graduation present, so there's *no* chance he'll be at Jeff's tonight."

"I don't care," I said, trying to sound firm but feeling weaker by the second. I hated hearing Josh's name spoken out loud, as if it somehow solidified his permission to exist in the same air I was breathing.

"Okay," Ethan said lightly, pretending to believe me. We walked in awkward silence for a few more seconds until I saw Carter and my parents at the edge of the parking lot.

"Carter!" I yelled, the life flooding back into my body when he looked at me. I ran toward him, letting Ethan's arm quickly fall off my shoulder.

"Congratulations, Ms. Cavanaugh, high school graduate!" Carter boasted as he embraced me. He tightened his hold and spun me around a couple times before safely setting me down. "And you, too, man." He motioned toward Ethan, who had caught up to us by then.

"Yep. I'll see you guys tonight. I'm gonna go find my mom," Ethan said with a forced smile that I didn't have the energy to analyze.

"My baby girl is all grown up!" my mom squealed as she came in for a bear hug.

"Mom!" I said as my face flushed.

"Oh, your boyfriend doesn't care, honey," my dad said with a laugh. "He's put up with us for this long."

"I think it's sweet," Carter replied. "You're lucky you got stuck with these two." He gestured to my parents, who were beaming.

"Boyfriend" was a term I still wasn't used to when referring to Carter Wells. He could have had anyone he wanted, so every day with him felt like this thrilling borrowed time I didn't quite deserve.

We made our relationship official late last summer after the dust settled from his breakup with Sloane Davison. She was blindsided by the news, as was everyone in our small town who had looked to Carter and Sloane as the royal couple of suburban Michigan. Nobody seemed to sympathize much with her, though. Apparently, her callous personality had rubbed too many people the wrong way over the years and, without Carter on her arm, most people lost their tolerance for all things Sloane. She quickly ran out of invitations and empathy.

When I heard she was transferring to a four-year college upstate, I wasn't surprised. I figured her only option was to start over with a new group of unsuspecting coeds who hadn't yet been burned by her relentless gossip and impatient eye rolls. Perhaps they'd be fooled by her perfectly manicured appearance as we had all once been, and she could rest on that for a few more years. But I was glad to have her gone, nonetheless. In the weeks following their breakup, Sloane had been a consistent drama source in Carter's life. There were drunken voicemails and unannounced visits. I was on constant edge that any one of her desperate attempts might just work, but to my relief and surprise, Carter was unwavering.

On sacred summer nights before the world knew about us, I'd crawl through his bedroom window, the nearby branches poking as he'd pull me to safety, laughing as I'd tumble inside, keeping our delicious secret safe for another night. And there was the moment he whispered that he loved me as we lay atop the grassy yard of a dimly lit local park, our bodies tangled over and under. The summer ended, but we swore we'd never forget.

After Sloane left, Carter and I started telling our friends that we were together. I wasn't used to it then, and a year later, it still didn't sound right. *Carter Wells is my boyfriend.* I couldn't say it enough.

The news spread quickly once our friends found out. "Who's the new girl with Carter?" people would whisper. I wanted to tell them that I wasn't new—I'd lived here all my life—but it was clear what they meant. I had been nobody for so long, I didn't blame them for being confused. The attention was daunting, but there was power in being loved by Carter Wells, and I got high off the validation. He was kind and generous and made me laugh harder than I knew was possible.

He could wear anything and make it look instantly trendy; the way fabric hung from his body was an art form. His thick, wavy, shoulder-length chestnut hair always smelled fresh, and his sharp jawline was intoxicating. His slender fingers felt like electricity against my skin and breathing in his sandalwood-scented aroma was like pulsing oxygen straight into my veins.

When he wasn't with me, I was lost in thought about his body, his face, his words, his allure. I was insatiably consumed by Carter, and the fact that *he* chose *me* was so overwhelming that I expected the emotional weight of that sentiment to crush me at any moment. I was buried under the inebriating anticipation and euphoria of being Carter's girlfriend. And I never wanted it to stop.

"We'll see you guys at home!" my mom yelled from her car down the row. They had driven to graduation separately from Carter.

As we settled into his old black sedan, he leaned over to kiss me after shutting the driver's side door. His lips felt soft but purposeful. I closed my eyes and felt the Earth spin beneath our feet as the clock ticked in steady, deliberate beats. Pulling back a couple inches, he kept his face close to mine for a moment as if he were studying my features.

"I'm proud of you, beautiful," he whispered. My skin tingled with the last word.

"Thanks, babe," I said sheepishly. I bit my lip to keep from throwing myself at him.

His deep mahogany eyes sparkled as he readjusted back to his seat. An exhilarating tension lingered between us as he started the car. I wondered if he felt it, too.

Chapter Two

As we pulled onto the road, I looked out the window, spinning deep into my thoughts as I often did.

"Have you decided if you want to go to Jeff's tonight?" Carter asked, his voice pulling me back into the moment as I settled into the passenger seat.

"Um, I hadn't thought about it much. Maybe? I don't know. Do you want to go?" I replied.

"I want to do whatever the graduate wants to do on her big day," he said with a smile, keeping one hand on the wheel and wrapping the other one around mine, interlacing our fingers as he drove.

"You probably don't want to go to a party with a bunch of high school seniors," I offered.

"Ahem, I think you mean high school *graduates*," he responded playfully.

"Ha, yeah, I guess I'm not used to that yet. But honestly, you humored me enough to come to prom. I don't want to force you into more high school stuff. That's the past, right?"

"I wasn't humoring you, Andie. I *wanted* to be with you. Trust me, seeing you in that black dress was more than enough reason to get me stoked about a prom."

"Ack, come on," I said, shifting uncomfortably in my seat. Whenever Carter complimented my appearance, I felt this weird mix of powerful joy and crumbling insecurity.

"About tonight, I'm down for whatever you want to do. Have you talked to Dr. Hawthorne about it?" he asked quietly, his eyes focused on the road.

"Yeah, it's fine," I said with a sigh. I hated that Carter knew I was in therapy. I felt like I had this flashing sign I wore on my body everywhere we went that read I'M MESSED UP in big, bold letters. I wanted Carter to find me mesmerizing and flawless, but his constant questions about my therapy sessions were regular reminders that that would never be the case. "She said I'm ready."

"What? That's fantastic, Andie! How do you feel?" he asked excitedly, which just dug my embarrassment deeper. It sounded like he was talking to a child.

"It's… I don't know. It's whatever. I know I'm fine because I don't even think about him anymore," I lied. Knowing that Josh wouldn't be at the party tonight, I continued boldly. "So even if he's there tonight, I don't care. I'm ready, and I know what to do."

"Great! And you know we can always leave if he shows up," Carter reassured me. I nodded.

"You know Ethan and the guys *will* be there, though," I said, referring to his ex-bandmates.

"Yeah … they're not my biggest fans right now, huh?"

"Well, Ethan said the other guys call me Yoko behind my back, so I don't think they're fans of mine, either. So you're in good company," I joked.

Carter had been the front man of Intentionally Blank, our town's local rock band. They were pretty well known at the regional level and had played all over the state. The guys had been like brothers, including Ethan, who was their drummer, and they were in the process of making plans for a Midwest tour when Carter announced he was leaving.

I was going to Columbia College in Chicago this fall, and Carter was coming, too. He had an old family friend, Jake, who had moved to the city a few years back and managed a popular pub named Blush that was located in the South Loop near campus. Jake promised Carter a full-time bartending job once we got settled, plus a cheap guest room to crash in until he saved enough to get his own apartment, but we figured most of our nights would be spent together, either in my dorm or at Jake's place.

When planning for my post-high-school life, my only priority was getting far away from where I was, far away from my past and the ghosts that waited for me in every corner of this old town. Everything was a reminder of Josh, my ex-boyfriend from junior year. My favorite restaurants were tainted with memories of his sharp, scolding tongue. The main roads were corrupted with flashbacks of empty threats and his unsteady laughter. My parents' house was dusted with foggy recollections of his belittling tone and heavy hands. Worst of all was the blue couch that stood unabashedly sturdy in the living room, mocking me from every angle, reminding me that I was one slip away from exposing my shameful truth to the world. That would be a surefire way to lose Carter and anything I'd been able to somehow hold onto since that day.

Carter thought he was my first, and I liked to pretend that he was, too. Sometimes I could even briefly convince myself that it was true. If I ever told anyone what had really happened on the blue couch that hot summer morning before senior year, I could lose everything. If my parents found out, they'd want to press charges, but I knew I wouldn't survive the questions or publicity that a trial would bring. If Carter found out, he'd know I had lied. And even if he could forgive the dishonesty, he'd never look at me the same. He didn't see me like the pathetic, violated girl I really was, and I would do anything to keep it that way. Carter cherished me as this pure, innocent, doe-eyed presence, and he, more than anyone, deserved to be protected from the truth.

I felt a little guilty that Intentionally Blank was breaking up so Carter could join me in Chicago, but they didn't realize how much I needed him. My sanity depended on his reassurance. His perfect hair and signature half-smile were life-affirming, and his constant attention gave me purpose. Part of me waited every day for him to realize he deserved so much better than what I could give him, and the other part of me desperately required his affection just to survive. It was a paradox that I could barely stomach.

"I told them they could come to Chicago, too, ya know?" Carter said. "It didn't have to be the end of the band. I don't know what they think is gonna happen if they stick around here forever. It could be a great opportunity for us to get noticed in a bigger city, but I don't know—I guess they just aren't ready to uproot yet..." he trailed off.

"You'll meet *new* musicians out there!" I offered. "Chicago has a killer music scene. Think of all the acoustic solo open mics you can do at Blush and wherever else, and the millions of clubs downtown that hire local talent. And trust me, I've known Ethan forever. He'll come around. Just give him some time to cool off."

"Sure, yeah, I know," Carter said, giving my hand a quick squeeze. "So, Yoko, may I escort you to the party tonight?" He smiled.

"Not funny." I laughed. "But, yes, Mr. Wells. Yes, you may."

****

"Andrea, honey, are you sure you want to go to this party?" my mom asked worriedly. "You don't have to go. Carter, tell her she doesn't have to go."

"You don't have to go," Carter repeated.

"Guys! Please. I swear I'm fine," I tried to reassure them.

"If he shows up…" my mom started.

"Mom! I know! Trust me."

"Don't worry, Mrs. Cavanaugh. If Josh is there and gives Andie any trouble, or even if she's just uncomfortable, we'll leave," Carter replied.

"Ugh, okay, promise you'll call me if you need me?" my mom begged, her arms folded tightly under her tense shoulders.

"Promise," I said, wanting to crawl out of my skin and trying not to visibly wince at the sound of Josh's name. "I'm eighteen now, Mom. You don't have to worry about me like this."

"I will *always* worry about you like this," my mom said, stiffly brushing a wisp of hair from my face. I shook off the touch and stepped back. "It's my job," she stated plainly, standing on the doorstep in her plush white monogrammed bathrobe as I turned around, heading toward Carter's car in the driveway. He playfully shrugged his shoulders and smiled at my mom as he trailed behind me.

I rolled my eyes. "Okay, Mom. Love you. I'll be back by curfew."

"Be careful, Andrea! Carter, please drive safe!" she pressed.

"You got it," he replied as we finally settled into the car. "Phew, has your mom always been this … involved? I mean, don't get me wrong, she's the sweetest. But I'm surprised you even told her we were going."

"I don't know. I've always been pretty open with them," I said, my mind immediately thinking of all the things I would never tell my parents. They knew that Josh was bad news. They knew he had cheated on me last year. They knew he was narcissistic and unkind, and Dr. Hawthorne had helped me open up to them about some of his more outwardly abusive behaviors, but even she didn't know about the blue couch.

"That's cool. I guess my dad's kinda the same way. But I'm twenty-one, so he sorta *has* to be chill about everything." He laughed. "And him working the night shift usually made this kind of thing easier when I was your age."

I bit my lip at the sound of those last two words. It was like I was only old enough for the world when it was convenient, or it wanted something from me. But every other time, I was just a kid.

"Anyway, let's do this," Carter said, sensing my tension as he started the car. "Do we know this guy, Jeff? The one who's hosting this party?"

"Um, not really. I think he ran track?" I guessed, grateful for the topic change. "But he lives in one of those big houses by the lake, and I heard his parents are out of town, at his sister's college graduation out east, or maybe it was his brother. I don't know. But it's become like the unofficial official graduation party for my class, so it should be pretty big."

"Right on," Carter replied as we drove down the dark neighborhood streets.

"Hey, I've meant to ask," I started. "Have you talked to Jake recently about that bartender job at Blush? It'd be perfect since it's so close to where we'll be living. I bet they make good money, too, since it's right by campus. Maybe he could get me a part-time job, too? Hostess or something?"

"Uh, yeah, I talked to him the other day. I still need to do some more digging."

"Okay, just keep me posted. Man, I can't wait to get out of here," I said with a sigh.

"You're *really* ready to leave, huh?" Carter asked.

"Is that a joke?" I snapped, instantly regretting my tone. "Sorry. I just mean, yeah, babe, it can't come soon enough. The only thing that got me through senior year was counting down to getting out of here with you. You're the only thing left about this town that matters. And with you in Chicago with me, this place can go to hell for all I care."

"Wow, strong words," Carter said quietly. "I mean, we grew up here. Don't you think you'll miss some of the little things? Or your parents? Your friends?"

"I'll be back for the holidays. My parents and friends will visit. And no, I don't think I'll miss the little things, or the big things, or the medium things. All I need is you. And to be away from here."

Carter smiled meekly and put his hand on my knee as he drove. He didn't understand, and that was okay. I didn't need him to. All I needed was for him to come with me so we could put every speck of Josh that hung in the bones of this town behind us. Even if Josh never came back, it didn't matter. He had already ruined this place. Everything here screamed at me to remember him. And all I knew how to do now was run.

Last summer, Josh was accepted into a prestigious private music school for his senior year. He was a piano prodigy with wealthy parents, so it made sense that he'd end up at River Academy. Nobody with much talent or money stayed in Oakwood for long, and he had both. Having Josh be hours away during the school year was like a sweet, sweet gift from the universe. And as far as I was concerned, it definitely owed me one, so I gladly accepted. He was gone, but he was everywhere. I hadn't seen his face in almost a year, which I thought would solve everything. Still, his essence was burned into every corner of the school and the town and every house and street, so the next step was to escape the surroundings and hopefully leave Josh burning in the wreckage behind me. When I looked at Carter, I saw only peace. His captivating radiance calmed me and scrubbed my mind of the darkness. So I figured that the brilliant combination of Carter and Chicago would be what finally saved me, and maybe then I could really move on.

Chapter Three

"Damn, this place is packed," Carter said, motioning to the long, narrow lines of parked cars creeping down Jeff's windy neighborhood road. "I think the house is way up there. Care for a walk?" He chuckled.

"I'm down. Oh, and I don't mind driving home if you want to drink," I offered.

"No way! You're the one with something to celebrate. I'm more than happy to drive," Carter said.

"No, I don't feel like it tonight. It's totally cool."

"Andie, you should really—"

"Stop, please. I don't want to." I didn't mean to cut him off, but I didn't want to talk about it anymore. I had made a vow to myself that I wouldn't drink again. I was never much of a drinker to begin with but had indulged a few times with Carter last summer. I blacked out once, and that was enough to scare me into stopping. There were too many things I needed to make sure I never said out loud, and there were people I needed to ensure I never called or texted. I had to stay in my right mind to keep the darkness deep down where it belonged. Drinking was too risky.

"Okay, then," Carter replied.

We got out of the car and started walking down the dark road. I took Carter's hand, forcing my fingers in between his. He gave mine a squeeze and let go, wrapping his right arm over my shoulders instead.

"There's Ethan's car," I said, pointing to the beige sedan with a broken taillight and dented bumper.

"Damn, this neighborhood is *nice.*" Carter changed the subject. "Can you imagine living in one of these houses?"

"Yeah, pretty crazy," I said. The air was cool, and Carter's red hoodie felt soft and clean against me.

The noise from inside was already pouring onto the front lawn as we stepped up to Jeff's front door. There was hip hop blaring from the TV speakers and slurred, excited chatter bouncing from every side as we entered the statuesque lake house. The large front room reeked of hard liquor, and the giant bay windows toward the back showed off a long porch that crept down to a dock atop a vast, dark lake.

"Wow!" I shouted over the commotion. I recognized Jeff barreling down the stairs.

"Hey, what's up, guys!" he shouted with a beer in his hand. "Come in!"

"Nice digs, man!" Carter said.

"What? You gotta speak up," Jeff yelled.

"I said 'nice digs, man!'" Carter raised his voice to match Jeff's elevated tone.

"Oh, thanks! Wait, whoa! You're Carter Wells, right? Mad respect, bro. I'm a *huge* Blank fan. Is it true you're breaking up?" His eyes were glassy as he steadied himself against the oak banister.

"Thanks, but yeah, haha, I think I might need a few of those before I answer that." Carter pointed to the beer in Jeff's hand.

"Oh, of course! Say no more!" Jeff stumbled over his feet to reach the cooler in the kitchen. "How about you, partner?"

"I think he's talking to you," Carter said, nudging me.

"Partner? Um, no, I'm good," I said, confused.

Jeff brought back two cold cans, opening one for himself and one for Carter, who nodded his appreciation and took a long, slow sip.

"Yeah, partner…" he said, his head tilting at my

puzzled expression. "As in lab partners. Chemistry class…"

"Right, of course, I'm so sorry," I said, having no idea what he was talking about.

"You're breaking my heart, Andrea!" Jeff said through laughter. "Am I really so forgettable? We graduated like two seconds ago!"

"No, no, sorry," I stammered. I fought to remember Jeff's face next to me in chem lab but couldn't place it. I'd tried so hard to just get through the year, I guess Jeff was collateral damage. I wondered what or who else I'd missed but quickly pushed the thought aside.

"Carter, you come to find me when you're ready to talk. Blank, man. I have questions about that last album that need answers!" Jeff yelled as he moved back into the crowd. Carter raised his beer in affirmation.

"You okay?" Carter asked me.

"Yeah, I think so," I said, shaking my head. "I'm fine. You? I hope this night doesn't turn into a whole guilt trip about the band breakup."

"Yeah, I'm good." He took another sip and pulled his car keys out of his pocket, placing them in my hand. "I think I'll take you up on that offer to drive tonight. Thanks, babe." He kissed me on the cheek and beelined to the cooler.

Red skirt. Black boots. Gold bracelet. Carter's in the kitchen. Josh is on another continent. I'm safe.

"Lovey!" Stephanie screamed when she saw me. "You made it!" She came in for a sloppy hug, her plastic cup sloshing as she moved. "Where's Mr. Andie?" she slurred.

"Carter's in the kitchen." I pointed. She turned to look.

"You sure?" she said, laughing.

"Oh, he was. He's here somewhere." I scanned the crowd but didn't see him.

"Well, good." She slung her arm over my shoulder. "Walk with me, girl. We got plenty to talk about."

I rolled my eyes, feeling suddenly too sober for whatever Stephanie wanted to discuss. I started regretting my decision to come to this party at all.

Stephanie flopped onto an oversized floral couch in the living room and patted the spot next to her. I carefully wedged myself against some other people I vaguely recognized from the school hallways.

"So, Chicago! You must be excited," she blurted. Her lipstick-stained cup balanced unevenly in one hand while her other hand rested on my shoulder. Her touch felt heavy and itchy, and I tried to wriggle myself out from under it. *Please stop touching me*, I thought. I couldn't get the discomfort out of my head, but her drunken density didn't pick up my cues, and she doubled down, gripping my shoulder. "I'm stoked for you, girl. You're gonna kill it at Columbia."

I suddenly became hyperaware of the person sitting behind me as their back rubbed slightly against mine with certain movements. I inched closer to Stephanie to get away, but that only encouraged her to pat and rub my arm as she loudly droned on about college. I couldn't listen. Each ounce of energy I had was spent figuring out how to get everyone to stop touching me. Her fingers lightly tapped my forearm as she talked, and the anxiety began to swallow me. The thoughts weren't linear or logical. I just needed these uninvited touches to stop before I imploded.

"What do you think your roommate will be like?" she asked. "I hope she's—"

I stood up abruptly, knocking her drink into her

lap in the process. I buried my head in my hands, sinking back onto the couch.

"Ugh, Andrea, what the *hell*?"

"I'm so sorry, Steph," I stammered.

"Why did you *do* that? What is *wrong* with you?" she screamed as she pulled some tissues out of her purse, dabbing her lap.

"I just, I'm sorry, you just wouldn't stop touching me," I started.

"*Touching* you? Jesus Christ, Andie, grow up," she snapped. "I was just *talking* to you! Forgive me for touching my best friend's arm during a conversation. God!"

I looked around, but nobody seemed to be paying attention. The atmosphere was so loud already that our outburst had barely caused a stir amidst the crowd. I felt another hand on my shoulder, and I whipped around, raising my hands up instinctively and closing my eyes.

"Baby, it's me. It's okay," Carter said. Recognizing his voice, I exhaled and opened my eyes. "What happened?" He pulled me up from the couch and embraced me. I buried my face into his soft hoodie, wishing I could just disappear into him.

"Oh, so *he* can touch you? But nobody else can get near you, is that it?" Stephanie shouted. I pulled away from Carter to face her.

"It's ... it's different with Carter," I said.

"Of *course* it is," she mocked. "Thank God for Carter Wells, the savior of Oakwood."

"Whoa, what is that supposed to mean?" Carter replied sharply, stepping in front of me.

"You know exactly what I mean," Stephanie hissed. She had always been bold and forward, which were things I loved about her, but I'd never been on this side of it before, and the alcohol only fueled her courage.

"Look, it *sucks* what happened to Andie last year, okay? Nobody denies that. Josh is a fucking asshole. I hate him more than almost anyone. I lost my best friend for a long time, and she lost herself in Josh. But instead of dealing with it, she just turned around and lost herself in *you* instead. And yes, Carter, we all know you're very pretty and very nice, so nobody else will tell you this, but Jesus, you're *not* helping her. She's clearly *not* okay, and you're just letting her disappear all over again. But because you're nice to her, we're supposed to just let her go? I'm sorry, but I can't do that anymore."

Carter opened his mouth to say something, but nothing came out. His gaze darted around the room, searching for ammunition, but he found none.

"Please stop," I said, quietly at first, and then again louder. "You don't understand, Steph. I love you, but you don't get it. Carter is … my life."

"Exactly," she said bluntly, her energy coming down as she took a deep breath. "Exactly."

Carter's head dropped as he let out a sigh. "Come on, Andrea, let's get some air," he said in my ear, linking his arm under mine and pulling me toward the backyard.

"You know I'm right!" Stephanie shouted as we walked away, finally stopping when the summer air hit us. It was tinged with cigarette smoke and steam from the bubbling hot tub nearby.

"Are you okay?" Carter pressed.

"I'm sorry. I'm so sorry you got dragged into that. She's insane. She's just drunk. Don't listen to her."

"Don't worry about me, Andie. How did this all start?"

"I don't even remember. It's nothing. Just please ignore her. I love you. That's what matters. Once we're out of here, none of this will matter, okay? Just you and me."

He brought me in for a warm hug and kissed the top of my head. He pulled back slightly and placed his hand softly against my cheekbone, bringing his lips to mine. I felt dizzy with pangs of the surreal exuberance that released throughout my body whenever he kissed me.

"I love you, too," he said gently. "I do. But … you know there's more to your life than just me, yeah? You're gonna be okay no matter what. You know that, right?"

"*We're* gonna be okay," I corrected him.

He didn't respond immediately, and before I could push for reassurance, Ethan's voice cut the tension.

"Andie!" Ethan shouted with a big grin on his face. He was seated in the crowded hot tub and started to get out when he saw us. Grabbing a towel from the nearby deck chair, he stumbled as he moved. "Phew," he said when he finally planted himself by me, wrapping his left arm around me for a side hug.

"Come on, man." I laughed as the warm water dripped from his body onto my shirt. He shook his head quickly, so the droplets spritzed toward me as they flicked from his curly hair. Ethan snickered through his wide smile, his sky-blue eyes dancing.

"You all right?" Carter asked him. "How much have you had to drink?"

"Not enough to talk to you!" Ethan said, his words slurring through some forced laughter.

"Ah, okay, so it's like that? Let's talk another time, man, after you sober up. Maybe tomorrow," Carter offered. "I want us to be cool."

"I have an easy solution! Don't move away!" Ethan remarked. His tone sounded like he was joking, but there was truth buried behind the inflection that Carter picked up on, too. I shot Ethan a steely glare, trying with my eyes to get him to stop talking. I didn't need anything or anyone to give Carter a reason to stay.

"I'm gonna get you some water," Carter said. "Will you guys stay here for a bit? I'll be back in a few." I nodded.

"We'll miss you!" Ethan shouted mockingly. His body started swaying, and I grabbed his forearm to steady him.

"Come on, Ethan, let's go sit down in the grass over there." I held Ethan's arms as we lowered ourselves onto a soft grassy part of the yard, the noise from the party still buzzing in the background. Once he was planted, he flopped down on his back.

"I think I can literally feel the Earth spinning," Ethan said with a loud sigh.

"Haha, I think you're just drunk," I replied, stretching out next to him, our heads both facing the starlit sky.

Ethan turned his head to face me, his left cheek resting in the grass. I turned toward him.

"You'll be fine. You just need some water and—"

"Don't go," he said quietly, interrupting me.

"Huh? Oh, come on, you've got to stop giving me such a hard time for taking Carter away from the band. I promise you guys will find another singer."

"I don't care about that," Ethan continued, suddenly sounding clearheaded. "Don't go, Andie."

"You can visit us whenever you want. I know it's not the same, but we'll still text like every day," I reassured him.

"You're my best friend. It's always been us against the world, you know?" He paused and took a breath. "What if I still need you even if you don't need me anymore?"

Each sentence hung more resounding in the thick,

humid air as the guilt crept in, disguised as acidic, aching nausea. I squinted my eyes as if that would help me process, but all I saw was Ethan as he lay on the soft grass next to me. His smooth, chiseled face was lit by the twinkly outdoor lights in the tree above us, his pale eyes burning into mine with an earnestness I'd never seen from him before.

"I *have* to go. You know I have to go," I said, my voice shaking.

"What if I never get out of here?" he asked quietly.

"All you have to do is make the decision and start driving," I stated, hoping that if I said it out loud, it would make it true.

"It's not that easy for everyone, Andie, and you know it. We don't all have safety nets or parents with money. And some of us have responsibilities here. And friends."

"That's not fair," I protested.

"Are you even going to take a part of me with you? I can't shake this feeling that you're just going to disappear."

"Yo!" Carter's familiar voice rang out behind us, and I shot up to a seated position.

"Hey!" I said chipperly. He casually sat down next to us, crossing his legs and handing a bottle of water to Ethan as he cracked open a fresh beer for himself. Ethan slowly sat up, too, taking the water from Carter without making eye contact.

"Thanks," Ethan said softly.

My mind was racing, and I felt soaked in the unrest. I loved Ethan in this profound and endearing way, but if he loved me, too, then he would understand that I wasn't just running toward something glamorous or exciting; I was saving myself from the town and darkness that threatened to consume me with each tainted memory. There was no way we could laugh through this tension to get back to where we once were. We couldn't binge-watch dark comedies in my parents' basement or swap playlists of our favorite new music without tonight's conversation bleeding into every word, every movement. I'd wonder if he was resentful that I left. He'd wonder if I even cared about what I left behind. I prayed that he was too drunk to remember tonight. If so, I could forget, too. I could push this down where the other things I chose not to remember dwelled in my body. And I was good at keeping secrets.

I decided instantly that I wouldn't tell Carter about this. He didn't need any more reasons to reconsider coming with me, so this, too, went deep into my vault. I could examine my feelings later if I wanted to, but for now, it just needed to go away.

"It was hilarious," Carter said as I realized he had been talking. I forced a smile and a soft laugh, hoping that was the appropriate response to whatever story he told.

"I need to lay down for a minute," Ethan said dizzily as he settled back down to the grass, closing his eyes.

"Yeah, he's probably out for the night. Jeff said he had a *lot* to drink. We should get him out of here. He can crash at my place tonight," Carter offered. I agreed. "Okay, come on, big guy," Carter said as he swung Ethan's arm around his neck and pulled him up. "Little help, babe?" he asked. I grabbed Ethan's other arm and placed it around my shoulders to help prop him up.

"Ugh," Ethan groaned, half awake. It felt strange being this close to him, my head under his chin with his arm around my shoulders as Carter and I helped him walk toward the car. Ethan and I had shared probably a million hugs throughout our years of friendship, but this time the closeness felt different, clouded by my wondering if it would be the last time.

Chapter Four

The next morning, I woke up groggy, grasping for my phone on the bedside table. It was already eleven AM, and I hadn't slept well. As I stared at the time on my phone, I groaned, remembering Ethan's words from last night. My vault was getting heavier by the day. I quickly shot a text to Carter.

Me: **Everything go okay with Ethan last night?**

I hoped Ethan had just passed out and stayed silent. Carter responded quickly.

Carter: **I guess. I set him up in the loft, but he was gone when I checked this morning.**

Me: **Okay, well, thanks for taking care of him. You're sweet. I love you.**

My phone dimmed as I waited for his response, so I tapped it impatiently to keep the screen lit. By the third dim, I locked my phone and sat on the end of my bed. My stomach was knotted. I told myself that not receiving a "love you too" affirmation didn't mean anything, but the stabs of rising panic in my chest appeared to disagree. I took some deep, forced breaths.

I stood up, brushed my teeth, and started to get dressed. I could hear my dad mowing the lawn outside my bedroom window.

"Okay, if I put my shirt on first, before my pants, that means Carter still loves me," I illogically reasoned. I played these little magical mind games often, as if I had some kind of power to change the universe's direction with a single indicated action. I knew it was silly, but it made me feel better in the moment, so it became my own private habit.

I carefully pulled my shirt on, tugging it over my head and smoothing out the sides, followed by pulling on my black stretchy yoga pants, and then stood firmly grounded on the hardwood floor.

"He loves me," I said out loud as if to force the universe to pivot according to my preference. I somehow felt more balanced. Empowered by my nonsensical ritual, I grabbed my phone and texted Carter.

Me: **Can I come over?**

Carter: **Sure.**

I exhaled deeply, knowing that seeing him would tone down my nervous energy. It was much easier to analyze his every thought when I could read his body language instead of just staring at words on a small, digital screen.

I straightened my hair, dabbed on some concealer and Carter's favorite rose-tinted lip balm, and headed downstairs to the kitchen. I grabbed a diet soda from the fridge, a banana from the counter, and my purse from the floormat by the front door, tossing my phone into it amidst the assorted mess of receipts, hair ties, keys, and my leopard-print wallet. As I ventured outside to the driveway, I squinted against the sharp sunlight and flagged my dad down from the direction of the loud lawnmower. He paused and slid one of his headphones to the side, just enough to hear me yell that I was going to Carter's. He flashed a thumbs-up and continued. I figured my mom was at some church luncheon since it was Sunday, so I took the thumbs-up to mean I was free, for a while at least, without requiring further explanation. I settled into my car, reversing down the driveway, opening the banana with the one-handed maneuver I'd become accustomed to when rushing out the door.

I fell deep into daydreams of Chicago as my car practically drove itself to Carter's house, pausing only for red lights and quick sips of diet soda. There were tingles in my stomach when I thought about living with

Carter in a different city. I called these Carter-induced tingles my "lightning" because they were so much more than butterflies. If there had ever been lightning, Carter was lightning. He was this exuberant, bright flash that thrilled its spectators, like a force from the sky that drew you toward it despite the danger of getting burned. I daydreamed about introducing him to whatever cool new group of friends I'd make at college, having them wonder how I got such a masterpiece of a boyfriend while his arm fit tightly around me. They didn't need to understand. They just needed to know he was mine.

I dreamt about watching him perform in open mic nights at Blush, the crowd watching with their jaws dropped as the spotlight glistened against his dark, wild hair. "Wow," my friends would say. "I know," I would reply with a slow, confident nod. And then we'd go back to my dorm room, where we'd make love. He'd kiss my neck and tell me I was everything to him in some poetic way, and I'd melt into his skin, burying my vault somewhere far away, deep underground where it belonged, not there in that peaceful room adorned with love and lightning.

Before I knew it, I had arrived at Carter's house. Excitedly parking on the street, I walked quickly up the porch to the sliding glass door that led to the living room. Carter was sitting on the couch, tapping on his phone screen. His left leg was swung casually over his right knee, and a charcoal pencil was tucked neatly behind his ear, barely visible underneath his thick, loose curls. He was wearing a soft, fitted Radiohead t-shirt and loose grey slacks with the cuffs rolled up a few folds. He looked up when he heard me slide open the door, and he quickly set his phone on the couch, turning it screen-down. He hopped up and gave me a quick kiss.

"What's up, babe?" he said cheerily, running one

hand through his hair while tugging at the hem of his shirt with the other, taking a sharp inhale.

"You okay?" I asked. I couldn't place his mood.

"Yeah, great!" he said loudly. "Sorry, yeah, I'm great," he said again, quieter this time.

"Okay," I replied, unconvinced. I wondered if Ethan had said something to him last night, or maybe Stephanie's judgmental words were bothering him. But I didn't want to think about them today. I sat down on the couch behind him, stretching out my arms in his direction, inviting him to cuddle.

He slid down beside me, placing his phone on the floor. I nestled against him and kissed the side of his mouth, leaving a light, sticky, rose-tinted stain, which I brushed off with my thumb. He looked at me, his deep brown eyes connecting to my gaze and bringing the lightning back in my stomach. But just as quickly, he looked away and sat back, his arm on top of the couch instead of wrapped around me, so I pulled it onto my body where he let it rest.

"What do you want to do today?" I asked. "I was thinking we could make a list of what we're going to bring with us to Chicago and what we still need to buy. Everyone says we should get a futon for the dorm, but I don't know. Is that even a thing?"

"Uh, I think I already know what I need to get," he replied. "But you can make your list? I was going to finish this drawing I've been working on, so can we just hang out?"

"Oh, yeah, sure," I said, wanting to be agreeable. Before Carter could get up, I moved my head slightly and softly kissed his jawline. That was usually my indication that I wanted to be intimate. I didn't really care about the sex; it was actually kind of painful. I just loved the way it made me feel close to him. And I loved that he loved it.

After sex with Carter, I would feel high for hours from the sheer power of being the person that got to have sex with Carter Wells, the person he chose to be exclusively intimate with.

All the kissing and touching before and after felt like my reward for getting through the rest. I never told him that it hurt because I didn't want him to stop. Not having sex would be a surefire way for him to lose interest, and that was not a risk I was willing to take, so I pretended it felt amazing. When the dishonesty tugged at my guilty heart, I'd remind myself that there was *some* truth in that because I *did* feel amazing after, just not physically. Physically I felt sore and achy and sometimes even had spotty bleeding for a day or two after. But the validation and power that came from it was a rush I could barely contain, and I had grown to need it like oxygen.

He turned his face away from my lips. Confused, I cradled my hand gently on the side of his face, his dark stubble prickly against my soft palm. I pulled him back toward me, leaning in to kiss him on the mouth, more firmly this time. I felt his shoulders slouch under him as he returned the kiss, his soft, wide lips pressing into mine. I closed my eyes, breathing in his scent, mentally preparing my body for the next steps. But instead, he pulled away sharply, standing up and shaking his head briskly.

"Andie, I can't. I'm sorry, I just … I was *right* in the middle of this drawing, and I really want to finish it. That's all. Raincheck?" His half-smile gutted me. I brought my knees to my chest, biting my lip.

"Sure, of course. Are you okay? Is it me?" I asked worriedly, the lightning bolts turning into a familiar panic.

"Of course it's not you. I just want to focus today."

Carter had never turned down my advances before. My intuition was screaming, waving red flags in every direction, but I forced a smile.

"Okay," I said through taut lips, trying to be the sweet, agreeable girl that I was growing tired of, worrying now that I wasn't the only one.

Carter's phone chimed. He jerked his arm out to grab it, swiping it open and trying not to smile, his eyes aglow.

"Who's that?" I asked, harsher than I meant to.

"Huh?" he replied, typing on his phone without looking up. I heard the *whoosh* sound of his text sending, and then he locked his phone, slung it in his pocket, and met my gaze. "Oh, just an old friend from back in the day, just catching up. Hey, do you want to see the drawing I was talking about?"

I nodded and followed him toward his bedroom in the back of the house.

"It's Mauna Loa," he said, referencing the stunning, half-done charcoal drawing on the easel by his closet.

"It's beautiful, wow. What is Mauna Loa?" I asked.

"Oh, it's a volcano in Hawaii. On the Big Island, I think. It's one of the world's most active volcanoes. I wanted to make this black-and-grey interpretation of something so, like, explosive. Literally explosive. But drawn in this dull, understated way."

"Wow," I said again, feeling smaller by the minute. "That's really cool, babe. When did you start this?"

"Last week. I'm hoping to finish it today, or tomorrow maybe."

"Nice. Well, don't let me stop you!" I offered, plucking the pencil from behind his ear and handing it to him as a peace offering of sorts. He smiled and turned toward the canvas, his phone pinging from his pocket.

I stayed for an hour, mostly sitting on his bed, typing notes on my phone to plan my Chicago shopping list, trying to be non-distracting as Carter feverishly drew, his hands becoming more and more smudged with charcoal.

"Okay, well, I think I'm gonna head out," I said plainly, with undertones that begged him to ask me to stay.

"Cool, talk later?" he said, not looking up from the canvas. My heart sank.

"Sure," I offered, walking slower and slower toward the door, giving him ample time to change his mind. He didn't.

"Hey, babe?" he said, finally looking up.

"Yes?" I asked excitedly, stepping quickly back into the doorway.

"Don't forget you have that Dr. Hawthorne appointment tomorrow. I can swing by after, and we can grab lunch if you want."

"Oh. Right," I said, remembering I had canceled that appointment last week. As far as Carter knew, I had been working diligently in therapy twice a week. He knew I forgot one time and ever since then had made it a point to remind me, but the more he reminded me, the less I wanted to go, or the less I wanted to *need* to go. The sweet, optimistic girl that gets the perfect guy and lives happily ever after in the big city doesn't go to therapy twice a week. She's level-headed, calm, and breezy. That wasn't me, though, far from it, so I tried to just act the part sometimes and see how it fit.

The therapy appointments were helpful at first, but lately had felt more like I was going through the motions. I had told Dr. Hawthorne everything I was willing to say to another human, but there was a lot more there that I wasn't ready to talk about, that I'd never be ready to talk about, so my mentality had shifted from fixing it to burying it. And somewhere outside of Chicago was where I was going to leave it behind. So my attendance at therapy had been spotty at best, but I didn't think Carter would understand, so I kept that in the vault, too. I swore to myself I'd be more honest once we moved; I'd really let him in. But at this point, I wasn't sure I even knew what that meant anymore.

Chapter Five

A few days passed, and the panic hadn't turned back to lightning yet. I would've even settled for butterflies at this point, but they didn't come, either. The constant anxiety was suffocating, but every night when I X'd off the day in my desk calendar with a thick permanent marker, I felt some semblance of satisfaction to know I'd made it another day closer to Chicago.

Another day closer to my world both expanding and shrinking at the same time, expanding to new opportunities and skylines, but similarly enclosing to just being Carter and me, co-existing in a small room against the world, surviving on half-smiles and jolts of lightning. Maybe even with a futon. I just had to make it eight more brutally slow, long days until we got on the train and left it all behind. I had received approval for early move-in at Columbia since I'd signed up for some summer prep classes, so I was leaving a couple months before most of the other people from my graduating class.

I hadn't heard from Ethan or Stephanie since the party, and I was grateful for that. The tension that night might be just what we needed to make a cleaner break in eight days. It'd be a lot easier to get on that train without Ethan's crystal-blue, sad eyes following me or Stephanie cracking loud, passive-aggressive jokes about my life choices.

Whenever a tinge of sadness started rising to the surface as I thought about cutting ties with my two best friends, I shoved it into the vault where it belonged, soon to be buried along with every inch of Josh that lingered under my skin, every violent flashback, every dishonest remark I lovingly said out loud to keep me sane, and every shred of heavy shame and dripping guilt that clung to my bones, reminding me that nobody loves a broken girl.

I needed to take action to snap Carter out of the funk he was in, to bring him back to me, like how he was before that goddamn party. So the next night, I told him I had a surprise and wanted him to pick me up at eight PM. I didn't tell him where we were going.

I heard his car cruise into the driveway and waited for him to come to the door like he always did. Minutes passed, and my mom finally broke the silence.

"So, is he coming in? Or..."

"I guess not?" I said. "I'll tell him you said hi. Got to go. Love you, bye!"

"Oh, all right," my mom said awkwardly. "I feel like I haven't seen Carter in weeks. Tell him we need to do a big family dinner before you guys leave, okay?"

"Sure, will do. Bye!" I said from halfway out the door. As I walked toward his car in the dark summer night air, I could see his face illuminated from his phone screen inside the car. I opened the passenger door and sat down, leaning in for a kiss. He moved his face toward mine to let me kiss his cheek, not looking up from his phone.

"Old friend?" I asked in a helplessly annoyed tone, fueled by not wanting anyone to ruin tonight.

"Yeah, sorry, hey," he said, locking his phone and sticking it in the cupholder between our seats. "Where are we going?"

"Just drive." I smiled. "Turn left on Orchard, and then I'll direct you from there."

"So mysterious," he teased, backing out of the driveway.

"So, what's the latest from Jake? When do you start at Blush? Did you talk to him about me yet?" I asked excitedly.

"Yeah, uh, everything's fine, Andie. I'll get the specifics when it gets closer."

"It's in seven days," I said bluntly. "We are moving in seven days."

"Shit, really? I can't believe it's coming up that fast." He ran his hand tensely through his hair. "Okay, yeah, well, I'll talk to him soon."

"Yeah, you need that job, Carter. Please don't forget to get the details from Jake, like, tomorrow."

"You got it," he said assuredly. "Okay, I turned on Orchard. Now where am I going?"

"Go like a mile and then turn left at the light on Lincoln. We'll be close then."

"Ohhh, I think I know where we're going," he said, unable to hold back a small grin.

"I thought we could use a little refresher," I offered.

He wrapped his hand around mine, keeping one hand softly gripping the steering wheel. With his eyes steady on the road, he brought my hand to his face and kissed it. I loved the way his lips felt whenever they grazed my skin.

He didn't ask for any more directions, just followed his instinct until he pulled into the back of an old, abandoned movie theater. The parking lot was mostly overgrown with weeds, and the building had been boarded up for years, despite the sign out front boasting the "cheapest new releases in town."

Carter stopped the car, rolled the windows down, and turned off the engine. The dewy air felt cool, and I let out a deep breath. I took Carter's hands in mine and turned in my seat to look pensively into his luminous chestnut eyes.

"I wanted to bring you back here to remember when this all started," I said, motioning to him and myself. "Carter and Andie started here. Remember? Us, as us. When we made it official. We didn't want Sloane or anyone to find out we'd been seeing each other in case they thought you broke up with her just because of me, so we'd meet here to make out and talk and feel safe and free. The last time we came here was when we said we weren't going to hide anymore. We went from being two recently single people coming out of some toxic relationships to being us. Together. Whenever I pass this place or think of this place, I feel so, like, even more in love with you because I remember how it all started and how much it's grown since then."

He smiled at me sweetly, sincerely, silently.

"Ya know?" I asked, prodding him to talk.

"Yeah. I know," he whispered. His eyes glistened. He opened his mouth but closed it again before saying anything.

"Andrea," he said softly. My full name sounded strange in his voice. Before he could continue, the loud buzz from his phone vibrating in the cupholder startled us both. He dropped my hands to grab the phone, and as he did, I tilted my head to read the name on the brightly lit screen.

"Olivia Schroeder: one new message," I said out loud as I read. "Olivia Schroeder? Who is Olivia Schroeder?" I asked, confused.

"Just an old friend," he said dismissively, opening his phone to read the message before quickly locking it and setting it back down. It buzzed again. "Stupid vibration setting. Sorry." He turned it to silent. "There. Sorry."

"An old friend from, like, where?" I asked, still puzzled, hating how the name "Olivia Schroeder" sounded in my mouth.

"From a long time ago. She used to live on my

street when we were kids. Her family moved away in high school, and we're just catching up because she's back in town."

"Oh?" My eyes widened, and I pulled back, sitting up against the door. "Is this *the* 'old friend' you've been texting with non-stop? I guess I just assumed it was a guy. Why didn't you tell me?"

"Because it's not a big deal. Really. And I didn't want you to be worried about something that's not a big deal. Look, I don't even have to respond."

"Okay," I said, unsure of what to say next. "Have you like, *seen* her?"

Carter's eyes darted around the car as if he were looking for something to give him the answer to the question but never found it.

"Carter, have you seen her? Or are you just texting her?"

"I saw her. But she's just an old friend. That's the honest-to-God truth."

"Then why didn't you tell me?" I asked. My eyes started stinging, and my lips pursed. The panic was back, and this time it was infiltrating our special place. The summer air suddenly felt muggy against my skin, and I wanted to drive away, somewhere else, so as not to taint the memories of our sacred abandoned movie theater parking lot with words like "Olivia Schroeder."

"Because I didn't want you to think it was anything. Because it's *not* anything."

"So did you … lie to me? About a girl?" I asked, wiping a hot tear off my cheek.

"No, no, no, Andie, I didn't lie to you. I *never* lied to you. I just didn't tell you something. But you didn't ask, so it's not lying." It was clear he'd been telling himself this many times until it sounded rational. I knew that trick all too well. "Look, babe, I'll just delete the whole text conversation with Olivia, like it never happened, to show you how *not* a big deal it is, okay?" He opened his phone and swiped into their conversation, quickly scrolling through it. "I just need to find this one thing to save—the name of this band she told me about. I don't want to forget it because they were pretty good. Just let me get this name, and I'll write it down and then delete all of this. Okay? Andie?" He sounded frantic.

"Okay," I said, unsure what the right answer was, watching his hand scroll and scroll through what seemed like an infinite supply of text messages. My heart cracked a little with every swipe, seeing the many, many exchanges between Carter and Olivia Schroeder. He scrolled too fast for me to actually read anything, but the volume was enough to make me feel sick.

"Aha, got it. The Adjacent of the Lodged. That's the band. Cool name, right? Let me just copy that and paste it into my notes app ... okay, done. Done. Look, I'm deleting this whole conversation, Andie. ... And, it's done. Gone. All gone. See?" He showed me his phone proudly.

"Great," I said meekly, feeling nauseous. "I think I want to go home."

"Andrea, I'm sorry. I should've been more transparent with you. Really, I'm sorry. It won't happen again."

"How many times did you meet up with her?" I asked slowly, unsure if I wanted to know the answer.

He sighed and looked straight ahead. "Three times."

"What did you do?"

"Um, went to the beach at Lake Michigan once, looked at pictures from Hawaii, just mostly caught up since we hadn't seen each other in a few years."

"Hawaii?"

"Yeah, that's where she'd been living since freshman year of high school. Her dad's in the military."

"Hawaii. Mauna Loa," I said, feeling stupider by the syllable. "Of course. That charcoal drawing was for her."

"No, no, we just used to draw together back in the day, and she had this cool picture of that volcano, and it gave me the idea. Not *for* her."

"Does she know about me?" I asked.

"Of course," he said quickly.

"I just want to go home now," I said, needing desperately to get out of this parking lot. The place that had once been ripe with epic memories of giddy secret love was now stained with a different kind of secret.

We drove in silence, Carter looking worriedly between the road and my face, caressing my shoulder nervously. I buried my attention in my phone, shielding it away from Carter's view as I opened Instagram.

Olivia Schroeder, I typed into the search bar. The top result showed someone who had one follower in common with me: Carter Wells. I couldn't click fast enough.

My heart dropped when I saw her face. She was beautiful. Her profile picture showed a young woman with silky sun-kissed skin smiling under a sweep of dark blonde hair. Her lips were full, and her lashes were long. I hated her. I looked through her most recent pictures, one of her with another woman on a hiking trail, wearing only a sports bra and tight bike shorts, showing off her perfectly toned abs and petite athletic build. The next picture was some collage homage to Hawaii with sappy colorful words over old photos of palm trees and tropical landscapes.

When the third picture popped up, I nearly dropped my phone. In a black bikini on a familiar sandy beach, there was Olivia Schroeder, making a goofy face at the camera with her elbow resting on Carter's arm. He wore dark blue board shorts with no shirt, making an equally goofy face with a crinkled nose and silly expression. His hair shone in the sunlight, and they looked happy—like they'd been laughing for hours. The worst part of this picture was how much they looked like they belonged together, as if beautiful people should only be with other beautiful people, like it just made sense.

I scanned back to my own profile, looking at my latest picture where Carter and I stood together outside my graduation. I used to love this picture, but with fresh eyes, we suddenly looked rigid and out of place. He was dressed up, even though I knew he hated formal attire, tall and smiling, his arm tight around my shoulders as I beamed in my purple graduation gown. I stood blissfully unaware of the free-spirited man I'd trapped in a stuffy blazer beside me, celebrating something he'd done years before, posing with his young, naive girlfriend who lied to him about almost everything to try to be the girl she thought he wanted. I couldn't imagine what would happen if he found out my truth.

He belonged on a beach with a bikini-clad, outdoorsy girl with perfect abs and sweeping hair. Not in a scratchy tie with his teenage girlfriend who thought a seedy abandoned parking lot was romantic.

I knew that every second with Carter Wells was blissful borrowed time. In the beginning, he thought I was this haunting, innocent mystery he needed to crack, and now, a year later, maybe he realized there was nothing more to it. Part of me would be closed forever; not even Carter Wells had enough magic to find the key. And the rest of me was just not that interesting. At least my faux sanity had gotten me close to the sun, even if briefly.

How could I be this angry at Carter's omission of the truth when our entire relationship was sitting on a foundation of my dishonesty? I'd never tell him what really happened with Josh or the truth about the deep scars on my forearm. He'd never understand that bloodlet was a requirement for ridding my body of the poison that Josh left behind.

Ever since my relationship with Josh ended, everyone thought the worst was over and was thrilled that I was "free." So I let them. That seemed more comfortable for everyone to get on with their lives than to know the truth, that this was a life sentence, even if I never saw Josh again. I was different, and the scars on my arm gave me this sick insight into how bad it hurt to just be me. At least this way, I could see it.

I put my phone in my lap, staring out the window, knowing what was coming next and thinking maybe the car would just veer off the road before it happened. But it didn't. As we neared my house, Carter pulled over on the side of the road and turned off the car.

The silence was thick and deafening, and I waited in the dark for it to be official.

"I don't want to go," Carter said softly, staring straight ahead out the front window. "Andrea, I don't want to go."

Chapter Six

"You don't want to go where?" I asked calmly, knowing the answer but needing him to say it out loud.

"I don't want to go to Chicago," Carter replied, his eyes welling with tears. "I'm sorry, Andrea. I've been trying to find a way to tell you, but I just didn't know how. And I hate that this whole Olivia thing just happened because that has nothing to do with it."

I scoffed, tears streaming down my face that I wiped away aggressively, not wanting him to see me cry.

"Honestly, I felt this way long before I got back in touch with Olivia."

"Stop saying 'Olivia!'" I screamed, surprising even myself.

"Okay, okay," he said. His eyes were wild with fear and discomfort. I could tell he was lost, looking for me to make this easier somehow, but I wouldn't. Not anymore. If he was going to leave me to bury the vault alone in the darkness, to be isolated in this dense world where only his touch and scent and voice gave me the air to breathe, I would no longer play by the rules I had set for us. I would no longer be the agreeable, sweet girl. Apparently, she didn't get the guy, either.

"Do you not want to go to Chicago? Or do you not want to go to Chicago … *with me*?" I snapped.

"Both," he said quietly, looking down.

"How long have you felt this way?" I yelled, shooting him a fiery glare, hoping it would make him look at my eyes and feel the same crushing avalanche that I did.

"I don't know … a few months, maybe longer," he muttered.

"*Months*?" I screamed. "So you've spent these

last few *months* planning our move with me, telling me you loved me, having *sex* with me, all the while knowing you were never planning on going?"

He finally looked at me, his eyes sad and watery.

"What do you want me to say?" he asked.

"I'm going to start crying in a minute here, like really crying, and you do *not* get to see me cry over you, Carter!" I yelled, my voice breaking as I started to stagger out of the car.

"Come on, let me take you all the way home," he begged through shaky words.

"I'm like half a block away from home. I'm fine," I snapped. "Just please leave. Get out of here!" I screamed.

He put his hands up as if to say "I give up" and rolled the windows up, driving away, slowly at first. I stood on the sidewalk, watching his car get smaller and smaller until the gleam of his taillights disappeared. Only then did I feel it, all of it. The lightning had turned on me, and I felt it stabbing under my ribs. I crumpled to the ground, gasping for breath between choking sobs. I clasped my hand over my mouth to try to quiet my cries so as not to alarm the neighbors. Instinctively, I pulled out my phone and clicked on Stephanie's name.

"Hey, stranger!" her peppy voice greeted me.

"Where. Are. You," I said between gulping breaths.

"Andrea? Are you okay?"

"*Where. Are. You,*" I said again, feeling stuck in this endless, looping blur.

"I'm doing my nails with Cassie. Why? What's wrong?"

"Carter. Broke up. With me." I gasped through the stale air. "Come get me. Please." I hung up the phone and looked at the nearest house number, texting her the address where I was.

I stayed seated on the sidewalk while I waited for Stephanie, trying desperately to breathe between sobs. I didn't understand how something could hurt so bad when I knew it was unavoidable. I had *always* known Carter wouldn't be mine forever. That picture of him with Olivia Schroeder at Lake Michigan kept flashing in my mind. That picture made sense to me. It put the pieces together. I had wanted him to be only mine when he had always belonged to the world.

Carter deserved better than me, and I think everyone knew it except for him, so I just enjoyed every sweet second until my allure inevitably dulled and he found better ways to spend his time. And when he rekindled this connection with a beautiful girl who came from an exotic island and loved art and hiking and was his same age and recommended cool indie bands, that was probably enough to push him over the edge to realize that it was never me. Maybe I was just the excuse he needed to finally leave Sloane last year. Or perhaps he just wanted to try living a simpler life with a simpler girlfriend who hates hiking and can't draw but worshiped every step he took and hung on his every word and memorized every syllable to every song he wrote.

It didn't matter, really, though. Whatever his reason was, I had gotten a year of Carter Wells, even though I didn't deserve a day. I almost convinced him that if I just loved him enough, that would be enough to make a life out of. We both knew it wasn't, but man, I got close, I think. The fact that I once got to see a mountain look small, to hold it in my hand, that I brushed against lightning and had the charred lungs to prove it, that I stared fearlessly into the sun and for a fleeting moment it met my gaze … that mattered. But now, the heartache swallowed me on that sidewalk. I had been eviscerated by five words. "I don't want to go."

Finally, I saw Stephanie's car pull up and heard the car door unlock as she emerged wearing a velour tracksuit over a white ribbed tank top and flip flops that showcased her smudged, half-done pedicure. She slammed the door behind her and overpowered me with a bear hug.

"I'm so sorry, Andie," she whispered as I fell into her. "I am so sorry. Come on, get in, let's go to my house."

I nodded, and she helped me into the car. We drove in silence except for the low hum of Fiona Apple coming from her car stereo. I stared out the window, slumped in the passenger seat as we drove the short distance to Stephanie's house. Once we got into her bedroom, I finally looked at her with weary, red eyes and a defeated stature.

"What happened, hon?" she asked gently, handing me a box of tissues. I told her the story.

"Well, I'm sorry to ask this, but are you sure that you're, like, actually broken up? It just kinda sounds like maybe he didn't want to move, but did you get actual closure? Are you maybe gonna be together long distance? Or would you stay in Oakwood if he said you could be together if you didn't move? Or...?"

"No," I answered quickly. "I can't stay. That is not an option. But being long distance, or whatever ... I don't know," I wondered aloud. "It feels like it's over."

"Right, but are you *sure*?" she asked. "Honestly, Andie, if it were me, I'd just want to know for sure. Take any guessing out of it." She picked up my phone and handed it to me. "You deserve to know."

I nodded and took a sharp inhale, clearing my throat. Stephanie put her index finger to her mouth to show me she would be quiet while I was on the phone. I called Carter and felt instantly sick when I heard the ringing. After a few trills, he picked up breathlessly.

"Andrea? Hello?" he asked worriedly.

"Hi," I said, trying to stay as emotionless as possible.

"How are you?" he asked, which felt cruel.

"When we talked tonight, it was clear that you didn't want to move. I understand that now." I talked slowly, methodically, every word draining my body of more energy. "But it isn't clear, actually, what that means for our relationship."

"Oh, Andie," he said sadly. I knew the answer. I'd known the answer ever since the day I met Carter Wells, but Stephanie was right. I needed to hear him say it, or I'd be left with a lifetime of "what ifs."

"I need you to tell me," I said. "If you ever loved me, even if it was a long time ago, or if you at least just cared about me, you'll be honest with me right now."

I heard him sigh deeply and sniffle. The pause of silence burned like a gaslit flame, taunting me as if I were remembering us wrong, like maybe we'd never happened at all. Maybe he was just this holy land I had only met in a dream.

I closed my eyes and flashed back to last winter when I drove through a blizzard with a broken windshield to see him. I'd had to crane my neck out the frozen window to trek the miles that stretched between us because not going was not an option. The risk was worth it. It always was. In another flash I remembered the time he looked small to me once, only once, sitting on the countertop, hunched over, nervously biting his soft lip. Nobody else was home that night, and he waited for me to kiss him. His eyes were impatient, and his wild hair aglow with streams of moonlight that poured in from the breezy open kitchen window.

He was lust and power and I'd shield my eyes when he came around, desperate to make him laugh, praying I was worthy enough to leave a mark. But that night he was mine, and I kissed him like I meant it because, God, did I mean it. But now I was questioning everything. He had been dreaming of others when I dreamed only of him. I had let him in and set up furniture there, but I'd lost him somewhere in the field we once floated through.

"I don't love you, Andrea. I am breaking up with you."

Despite my best efforts, hearing those words delivered so clearly just solidified the truth that I was unlovable, and my facade began to crack. This might be the last time I spoke to Carter Wells.

I knew my place here. I would never be Olivia Schroeder. I would never be good enough for Carter, so there was no point in fighting it. My mind scrambled at what the right thing to say would be, what might be my final words to the man who brought me back after I thought Josh had slipped me into the darkness for good. But it wasn't Carter's job to hold me up. He didn't need that burden, especially when girls like Olivia Schroeder were there to offer him all the light without any of the darkness. I hadn't let him shine when he deserved only to shine. Carter was nothing but illumination.

"Well," I said, disappointed in my voice for breaking. "You have broken my heart."

I hung up, shaking my head at Stephanie, who embraced me again, letting my head rest on her shoulder while I sobbed. This time, her touch felt warm, welcome, and necessary. This time, there was no Carter left to fill my need for human touch when I left Stephanie's house. So she just let me cry and stroked my hair. And I let her.

Chapter Seven

My eyes opened heavily the next morning to the hazy reality that came with being single again. It hadn't been a bad dream. Carter had finally left me. He had escaped to live a new, fresh life, free of whatever I was holding him back from. Or maybe he just needed to be free of me, free to make goofy faces with girls in black bikinis without the weight of upsetting the plainer girl back home, the one who was uncomfortable wearing shorts in public, let alone a bikini.

I wondered how he woke up this morning. Did he feel guilty? Did his heart ache, too? Or was he able to exhale for the first time in a year? Had he told his friends that he was planning on leaving me? Had they laughed at how clueless I was for the months that he knew? Did he care that I would be lost without him? Or was that pressure why he left in the first place?

I heard my mom bustling in her room across the hall, getting ready for work, so I slunk in and sat down on her bed.

"Oh. Hey, Andrea, I didn't even hear you come in. How're you feeling? Six more days!" she said excitedly as she searched her vanity for the right necklace. "I see you've been packing. That's good. How much do you have left to do?"

"He's not coming," I said quietly.

"Who's not coming where now?" she asked distractedly.

"Carter's not coming to Chicago. With me. He broke up with me last night." The words tasted bitter behind my teeth.

"Oh my God," my mom exclaimed. Her eyes widened as she hurriedly sat down next to me. "Honey, I had no idea. I don't even know what to say. I'm so sorry. What happened?"

"He just … told me he didn't love me," I said, looking down at my hands.

"Oh, Andrea, he doesn't know what he's missing. This is *his* loss. You know that, right? He's probably just scared of moving and everything. It just wasn't meant to be. You will be okay. I promise. Now tell me what happened." She stood up and walked slowly into my room while I repeated the story I hated telling.

I followed her as I talked. She nodded and gave the occasional affirming "mm-hmm" as she moved around my room, quietly taking some picture frames off my desk and placing them neatly into drawers, softly pulling certain items out of my suitcase and shoving them aside. She was silently ridding my life of Carter Wells. There was the moody black-and-white picture I took of him where his windblown hair fell over his forehead, the painted postcards he made with my favorite poems adorned to the front, the scarf he wore on stage that smelled perfectly of his salty sandalwood sweat; she was sweeping it all aside, and I was letting her.

I couldn't do it. I wouldn't. So I let her rip off the Band-Aid while she pretended to listen. I slowed down my words to give her more time. One item after another, the atmosphere was being absolved of all things Carter. If only it were as easy to delete him from everywhere else, too. But I knew the world was better with him in it, even if he wasn't mine.

Part of me stupidly thought that maybe we'd really run away together. Like maybe if I could hold him tighter than anyone else ever had or could, it would mean something. For a while, I had thought that maybe Carter was better than distractions like black bikinis and empty Hawaiian promises wrapped in very shiny packages. But maybe nobody was immune to the glitter. Maybe nobody could resist the kind of gleam that blinds even the starriest of eyes with the best intentions. Carter Wells was the best man I'd ever met, but he was still just a man.

"I have to get to work," my mom said as she embraced me. "You'll be okay, Andrea. It's better that you found out before you moved. Now when you're at Columbia, you'll be there as, well, a young single woman. The world is yours now."

I nodded, but she didn't understand. The world *had* been mine until last night when it fell apart around me.

When I finally heard the front door close and her car start, I sank back onto my bed, staring at my phone and trying to stop wondering what Carter was doing. I had the urge to text Ethan and tell him everything, let his long arms comfort me, let him tell me I was going to be okay. For some reason, it always made more sense when Ethan said it. But I didn't know if he remembered our conversation from the party, and I couldn't risk letting him think I was somehow leading him on, like "hey, now that *I'm* miserable and needy, let's ignore everything you said the other night and just hang out so I can feel better for a minute." Ethan deserved better. With me in Chicago soon, he'd have a chance to find his own Olivia Schroeder and maybe even some semblance of happiness. I wanted that for him.

I opened Instagram to see if Carter had posted anything or unfollowed me or untagged pictures, anything to remind me that he didn't love me anymore, but he hadn't. It was all still there as it had been. At least there was proof that we happened.

****

Groaning as I awoke the next morning from a

dreamless fit of sleep, I grabbed my phone from the nightstand. There were no missed texts, calls, or notifications. Instead, there was just a blank screen staring back at me, the latest sinking reminder that Carter was really gone. I'd been clinging to this senseless hope that he'd changed his mind somehow, or that he'd at least reach out to check on me, anything to let me stare at the sun again, even if I knew it was short-lived. But the deafening silence was worse than any cruel words he could've spoken.

It was ten AM, and I was scheduled for one final therapy session with Dr. Hawthorne in thirty minutes. I desperately wanted to cancel, but I'd skipped the last two sessions and really didn't want to shell out the fifty-dollar late cancellation fee. So I begrudgingly went through the bare minimum motions of getting ready before arriving at her office a few minutes late.

I'd barely sat down in the waiting room when I heard her office door creak open.

"I was worried you weren't going to make it again." Dr. Stacey Hawthorne peered around the door. "Come on back, Andrea."

I obliged, trailing behind her and flopping down on the large, cushy couch in her well-lit office adorned with diplomas, framed certificates, and modern art. There were dozens of manila files piled atop a scattered desk with a pink coffee cup that read FEMINIST across the front in big, bold letters. Her ash-blonde hair was strewn around her face, falling messily against her baggy black blouse. She settled into her rolling office chair and faced me, appearing tired but focused. Her kind, round eyes stayed fixated on me behind her black-framed glasses as she scrawled quick notes on the yellow legal pad she kept tucked close to her chest between scribbles.

"I'm happy you came. I was hoping to see you

before you went to college," she started. "Is everything okay?" she asked worriedly, leaning forward as she studied my puffy eyes. I shook my head and bit my lip, my fingers tapping quickly against each other as I scanned for a soothing pattern.

"Carter left me," I said, hating how small my voice sounded.

"Oh, Andrea, I'm sorry to hear that. How are you doing? What happened?"

I shook my head again. I regretted saying anything to her.

"It's fine," I lied. "I just ... that's why I probably look like this." I motioned to my disheveled appearance. "I don't think I really want to talk about it if that's okay. I just thought I should let you know."

"Well, thanks for telling me." She paused. "This must change your plans somewhat then, right? Are you still going to Chicago next week?"

"Yes!" I snapped. "Of course. Why wouldn't I?"

"Well, I know you were looking forward to moving there with Carter, so I wasn't sure if something changed."

"It's going to be different, but I still have to go."

"You don't *have* to do anything, Andrea," she stated calmly.

"Yes, I do." My foot started tapping incessantly, and I was losing track of the patterns my finger tapping had run through.

"Take a deep breath. Remember, you are safe here. Come on, I'll do it with you, deep breath in through the nose and out through the mouth."

I rolled my eyes and followed along, the exhale coming out in shaky, shallow bursts.

"Good. Now, what do you see? What's here in this room that you can focus on to ground you, to remind you that you're here in this moment, in reality, not the past or future?"

"Umm..." I scanned the room quickly. "Beige carpet."

"Great. What else?"

"Umm ... black blouse." I pointed to her top.

"Perfect. One more."

"Pink mug." I motioned toward her desk.

"Great. Now say all three and look at each one."

"Beige carpet, black blouse, pink mug," I said aloud, feeling my gaze steady on each item. "Beige carpet, black blouse, pink mug," I said again through an exhale. I felt a calm wave through my body as I focused.

"Okay, are you here in this room with me now?" Dr. Hawthorne asked. I nodded. "Good work. Okay, so you're still going to Chicago, but it's going to be a little different now. Different doesn't have to mean bad, right?" I nodded again. She tore a blank page from her yellow legal pad and rolled her chair over, setting it on the coffee table in front of me with a black pen. "I'd like you to write at the top here, 'What Do I Want,' and then think of anything you could want from your future, anything at all, like as if you have a magic wand, and write down a list here. You don't have to share it with me or anyone, but think of it as a vision board of sorts. I think it will be great for you to just be clear on what you want from this experience and why you're choosing to go, especially now that things are going to be a little different than you expected."

I started writing before I even let myself think.

1) To be like Olivia, 2) To be pretty, 3) For Carter to want me back, 4) To never get hurt again.

I shielded the paper from Dr. Hawthorne as I scribbled faster than the thoughts could form.

"Do you want to share what you wrote?" she

asked.

"Oh, umm, it's just about like, wanting to get good grades and be successful, make friends, that kinda stuff." I couldn't look at her as I stumbled awkwardly through the lies.

"Mmhmm, okay."

I spaced out for the next forty-five minutes while she talked about meditation, self-care, and anxiety-reducing tactics as I fantasized about my list. I wondered if Olivia *knew* how lucky she was to be that irresistibly shiny. I would've died to know what that felt like, to be the heartbreaker instead of the broken, to have the tan skin that glittered in the sunlight and the thick, wavy hair that fell perfectly against your chest, to have a beautiful man with a perfect jawline who sketched charcoal drawings of exotic mountains just to see you smile.

"Did you hear me?" Dr. Hawthorne asked as I snapped out of my daydream.

"Sorry, yep," I lied again.

"Okay, so you'll sign up for therapy at the student health center when you get settled, right? I've already called and given them the referral, so they should be expecting you."

"Uh-huh," I replied distractedly.

"It's really been a pleasure getting to know you this past year," she said as she stood up slowly. "I hope you'll stay in touch and maybe come back when you're in town. And you can always call if you need something in the meantime, of course."

"Thank you for everything," I said truthfully. "I really needed you last year when everything happened with … him."

"Josh?" she asked. I winced at the sound of his name. Even on another person's lips, it made the air just as toxic.

"You know, Andrea, there's no graduation here. We don't just wake up, and everything feels good again. We only have a daily reprieve, and we have to be willing to work for it. Anxiety and PTSD are very real and can be very serious if we don't take care of our mental health. You wouldn't ignore a physical disorder. Like if you had diabetes or a heart condition, you'd take your medicine and see your doctors, right? It's the same thing with our mental health. Just because it's less visible doesn't make it any less real."

"I said I'd sign up for therapy when I got there, so I will." My body ached to get out of the office. I despised hearing the dishonesty drip from my voice, but I hated the truth more. I had no intention of following through on these empty promises once I was in Chicago. All I could think about was leaving the past behind in a cloud of poisonous dust as I sprinted out of state to try on some new skins until I found one that made me whole. Talking about the past would only make it hang in the air longer than I could bear. So I would not be talking about it anymore.

Chapter Eight

The night before I moved to Chicago, Stephanie had come over for dinner with my parents and me to say goodbye. I walked her to her car in the driveway and froze when I realized she was expecting a hug. She wrapped her small arms around me, and I did my best to return the embrace with a swift, awkward pat on her back.

"You sure you're okay to go?" she asked, wiping away tears as she pulled back.

"Yes. I'm incredibly sure," I said truthfully.

"You'll text me when you get there? I want to know everything. I can't wait to come visit."

"Of course, Steph," I said. She gave my hand a squeeze, and I quickly pulled away. "Sorry," I mumbled. "Just nervous, I guess? I don't even know how I feel right now, like, excited maybe?"

"Sad that you're leaving your very, very best friend since first grade?" she said, laughing through her tears.

"Well, *obv*iously." I chuckled. "But you know what I mean."

"I know. I just can't believe we're here. My little girl is growing up," she joked. "But seriously, Andie. *This* is your moment, okay? Carter was not your moment. Trust me, girl, I know he was a big deal, but he's, like, an *Oakwood* big deal. You're a *Chicago* big deal. He *does* have nice hair, I'll give him that, but he is not the stars and the moon and the sky all wrapped into one. You are."

I wiped away the first of many tears that night and hugged Stephanie again.

"You are," I said.

"*You* are." She giggled. "Okay, I'm getting out of

here before this turns into more of a sob-fest than it already is. Text me tomorrow. I love you!" she yelled in a sing-song voice as she got into her car. I waved as she drove away. I took a deep breath, inhaling my last night of Oakwood and exhaling it all back out.

The next morning at the train station, my parents hadn't stopped crying since they woke up.

"My baby is going to college," my mom kept saying.

"This is it, Andie. We are so proud of you," my dad said sincerely, handing me the last duffle bag he'd carried in from the car.

"It's a three-hour ride," my mom reminded me. "The train stops at a station right in front of Columbia. They have buses for all the early admin students arriving today. An upperclassman named Annie is supposed to meet you and some other kids there to take you…"

"Mom," I interrupted. "I love you, but don't worry, we've been over this a thousand times. I know what I'm doing. I know where to go."

"My baby is going to college," my mom said again, touching my face as I pulled away.

"You will call us the second you get there," my dad stated. "And every day after that. Anything you need…"

"Day or night, I know," I said, itching to run, ready to bury my graceless heart in the rich Illinois soil and let it grow again from scratch.

After more long goodbyes, the time had finally come. As I walked briskly toward the train, the view from the corner of my eye of my parents clutching each other, waving exaggeratedly from behind me, got smaller and smaller. I cringed at their exuberance and cringed deeper when I thought about them driving home to an empty house, wallowing in whatever weird sadness must exist when you spend eighteen years growing a human and teaching them not to need you. So I didn't think about it.

After settling the logistics of baggage and tickets, I sat down in my assigned spot, kicked my backpack under the seat in front of me, and closed my eyes. I was alone. People were milling all around me, but I was profoundly and incredibly alone. The jitters in my stomach mimicked excitement, and my foot tapped nervously.

If I tap my right foot three times, my left foot two times, and then both feet at the same time, that means this was the right decision, I told myself. I obeyed the ritual, and my breathing calmed. *This was the right decision*, I thought assuredly. And as I felt the train start moving underneath me, the nerves melted more with every minute and every mile that separated me from Oakwood, Michigan.

I couldn't stop the smile from maniacally creeping over my face as I pictured all the places I used to go with Josh and how they were further away from me now than ever before and gaining distance by the second. That 24-hour donut shop that reeked of cigarettes and sugar would still be open tomorrow, but I would no longer be a short drive away from it, which meant the memories of Josh's angry quips and passive-aggressive comments he'd make through sloppy mouthfuls of cinnamon rolls would be far away, too.

But that meant that the memories of Carter's sweet words and funny stories over hot cocoa and chocolate eclairs would also be distant. As well as the pensive conversations I'd had with Ethan about dark comedy and alternative music while we sipped lattes and pretended we were grown up enough to like them. But now I was ready to make new memories at new diners with new people.

I took a deep, cleansing breath and stared out the window, noticing every tree, every detail of the air that swept me farther and farther from so many of my firsts and, hopefully, a lot of my lasts. There were now miles stretched between my body and that blue couch that mocked me in my parents' living room, the blue couch that knew my secret and stood sturdy beneath me that morning I lost myself for good. Or at least the version of myself that had existed in the world before Josh scraped it out of me, leaving me an unclean shell on a soft blue couch with no choice left but to run.

I now felt every inch that separated me from the fresh self-inflicted wounds that would momentarily remove the poison but left specks of blood on my sleeves as a bleak reminder. And if that meant I also had to put space between the good parts, too, then so be it, because the darkness would've swallowed me there.

Chapter Nine

When the train stopped, I stood up quickly, giddy from the high of being 172 miles away from my past and vowing to keep it there in that town of broken dreams and long winters. My eyes had widened with each passing of skyscrapers and trendy restaurants, so by the time we stopped, I was ready to claw my way out of this train car and feel the Chicago sun on my face, wondering if it would feel different. It did.

I barely remember the journey from the train to my dorm. It felt like I was floating above my body as I met the Columbia group at Union Station. I don't think I said a word as I followed the tall navy-blue flag sticking out of the guide's backpack, stumbling to keep up as I studied the campus, dragging my bags on a grey plastic cart with Student Move-In stamped to the front.

"Let's see … first dorm stop is The Dwight, which was recently renovated but still maintains its historic charm," the student guide read from an index card. "Luciana Ramirez, Malik Barnes, and Akani Ito, this is where you'll be living. Head inside and they'll be ready to help you in the lobby."

I'd been so enchanted by the modern surroundings that I'd forgotten there were other people in my group, making awkward small talk with each other and taking pictures as we'd walked. I'd never met anyone named Luciana, Malik, or Akani before. Their names sounded pretty as I repeated them in my mind. Suddenly the Carters, Joshs, Stephanies, and Ethans of the world felt so small. The group kept walking, and I followed blindly.

"Cavanaugh. Andrea Cavanaugh?" the guide said when we reached the next stop. "And Hannah Taylor.

You two get off here. We're on State Street, and this is the University Center, your new home. Check in at the front desk, and they'll get you set up."

My ears perked at the name "Hannah Taylor." According to the Residence Life department's letter earlier this summer, "Hannah Taylor" was my roommate. I hadn't learned anything about her yet since my living situation had always felt so defined by Carter. I figured if I got a bad roommate, I'd spend most of my time in Carter's room at Jake's apartment, or if my roommate was rarely around, maybe Carter would be at my dorm most of the time. But this was the first time I considered that I'd really be sharing a home with another person who I knew nothing about.

Hannah Taylor was beautiful. She was tall and athletic with smooth brown skin, and full lips softly painted with a dewy gloss. Her springy dark curls were pulled back into a tight ponytail, and her snug tank top showed off her toned, slender arms. She walked with confidence, and her wide smile showed off a bronze hue in her cheeks. I was mesmerized by her right from the start.

Hannah walked toward the tall, shiny building that was meant to be our new home, and I pulled my cart along to catch up with her, huffing under its weight as she walked quickly, purposely, without breaking a sweat.

"Hannah?" I said between breaths.

"That's me," she replied flatly.

"I'm Andrea," I said, finally matching her gait. "I think we're roommates?"

"Yep," she said as we walked through the sliding glass doors to the large, busy lobby.

"Taylor and Cavanaugh," she stated to the student behind the reception desk.

"Welcome to University Center!" the girl chirped.

"You'll love it here. I'm Amber. I live on the fifth floor. Looks like you two are..." she flipped through some papers on a clipboard, "*also* on the fifth floor. Yay!" Amber squealed. "Avani is the R.A. of our floor, and she's the best. You'll love her."

Hannah rolled her dark brown eyes, looking at me for the first time. I was vibing on Amber's energy but quickly realized from Hannah's raised eyebrow and quiet smirk that she wanted me to return the glance, so I rolled my eyes back and shrugged my shoulders. Hannah held back a smile, then looked at Amber, mocking her tone in an overly peppy voice.

"Super, Amber! Just tell us the room number, and we'll be on our way, girlfriend. Go, Cougars!"

Amber frowned, unamused. "Five-Seven-A," she said quietly, handing us each a welcome package. Hannah grabbed hers and moved her cart toward the elevator.

"Sorry," I mouthed to Amber with a grimaced face, gently taking my package and hurrying to catch up with Hannah.

"I swear, Cavanaugh, I don't know if I can take all the cheerleader hype that comes with the first day. Oh God, you weren't a cheerleader or something, were you?"

"No," I said, laughing at the thought. "Hardly."

"Great," she replied, eyeing me up and down in the elevator. "So, what's your deal exactly?" she asked. "You gonna be a chill roommate? Or a pain in the ass?"

I giggled uncomfortably at her bluntness. "Chill?" I guessed.

"It wasn't a pop quiz," Hannah stated.

The elevator dinged, and I exhaled some of the nervous energy.

"Guessing this one is Five-Seven-A," Hannah

said as we reached a plain door that had "Hannah & Andrea" written in bubble letters on silver construction paper taped to the front.

The room was small, with a bed on each side and two desks shoved in between them that sat under a window looking out over a sea of buildings. The walls were a pale yellow, and a full-length mirror was propped up against a corner.

"It's perfect," I said, loving that it was mine.

"It's fine," Hannah retorted as she began unpacking, pulling her mint-green sheets over the mattress.

"Where are you from?" I asked timidly as I unzipped my first bag.

"Green Bay," she replied assertively. I studied Hannah as she talked. She was nothing like Oakwood.

"Cool. I'm from Oakwood."

"Where?"

"Ha. Exactly," I said. "What's your major?"

"Interior architecture," she said proudly.

"Cool," I said in a subdued voice, trying to mask just how fancy and interesting I thought she was. "I'm thinking about journalism." I cringed when I realized she hadn't asked.

"You know it's hot as hell outside, right?" Hannah waved toward my dark wash jeans, long-sleeve tee, and thick pleather ankle boots.

"I guess," I nervously replied. "I just … like this."

"You like sweating to death?"

"I like coverage," I said honestly. Hannah squinted like she was trying to figure me out.

"Okay, Cavanaugh, I'll bite. What was your deal in Oakville or whatever the hell? You play sports? Party?"

I had practiced how I would answer this question safely. My priority for survival was to keep my past vague. I didn't want to lie, because that would be too hard to keep track of, but I had buried the horror somewhere in the 172 miles between Oakwood and Chicago, so I needed the perfect answer.

"Oh, a little bit of everything," I said. "You?" My other trick was to turn the conversation back to the other person. I found that people loved talking about themselves and would soon quickly forget about me if I gave them a pass.

"Mmhmm," she murmured. "We're not done with you yet." She smiled.

Yes, we are, I thought.

"I played basketball," she offered.

"Cool," I replied.

As we unpacked, we talked a little more in between phone calls that Hannah took from what appeared to be her many friends in Chicago. I texted my parents and Stephanie and tried to keep to myself as I went through each bag until the last one was empty. I looked around at my half of the room, satisfied at how perfectly plain it was; the blank canvas I had earned along with my freedom. It was a stark contrast to Hannah's side, already messy with strewn clothes, books, and jewelry she hadn't found a place for yet. There were twinkly lights woven around her bookshelf, animal-print throw pillows on her half-made bed, photographs of faces I didn't know taped over pockets of the wall, along with a stunning pop-art poster of Alicia Keys.

I sat gingerly on the end of my bed, unsure of what to do with myself in this newfound world. I had plans to do an official orientation tomorrow, scope out my summer class route before classes started next week, and see if I could scavenge a part-time job somewhere to pass the time and earn extra cash, but none of that started tonight. Tonight I was alone, without a to-do list, surrounded by people who knew nothing about me, with Alicia Keys judging me from the wall.

My antsy fingers itched to tap. *If I tap my thumb against my leg, then my middle finger, then my pinky, once on each side, that means this was the right decision,* I nonsensically told myself, obeying the forced ritual. *Okay. This was the right decision.*

I looked down at the blank screen on my phone.

"I will not open Instagram," I whispered out loud, knowing that the rabbit hole of Carter, Olivia, and other people who were happier without me would overshadow my new Chicago high.

"Hey, Cav, instead of opening Instagram, come out with me tonight," Hannah beckoned from her side of the room, not looking up from painting her toenails a metallic shade of teal.

I blushed, realizing that even my quietest form of self-talk was no longer private in this new, shared space.

"Thanks, but that's okay," I said, knowing she was just trying to be polite to the weird new roommate who wore black boots in the summer and came from who-knows-where Michigan. I curled my hands into fists instead of giving in to the longing to pick at the freshly healed scab on my forearm.

"Wasn't really a question. Just ditch the boots and the shy girl routine and come out. What else you gotta do tonight? Do you even know anyone yet?"

"Shy girl routine?" I asked softly, not realizing I'd been pegged for a stereotype already. I was hoping for "bold" or "mysterious" or something sexy and exciting, not "shy." I couldn't let that stick. The old Andie was meek and pathetic, standing in the back, hiding under eyeliner and loud friends, but I wanted the new Andie, the Chicago Andie, to be the one people noticed. I wanted to be Hannah Taylor so bad I could feel the envy-tinged admiration seeping from my pores. The unabashed way she entered a room, the way her voice never trembled when she spoke, the way she didn't have to try to be pretty because everything about her just sparkled with ease—it was unlike anything I'd seen before. I would do anything to have that confidence, to exude that kind of "it's in your best interest to be on my good side" aura.

"You know, the 'I'm from a small town and moved to the big city to reinvent myself' thing," she said.

Damn. Was it that obvious? I thought, feeling suddenly exposed and delicate.

"But it's all good, Cav," she continued. I liked that she had a nickname for me already. It made me hope that others would hear it and assume we were already friends. "You're in college now, so let's just leave that shit behind and start this thing right. When my nails dry, I'mma get dressed up right and head to this party at my friend's apartment down the block. You in?"

I nodded, wide-eyed.

"How do you already have a friend here?" I asked, genuinely wanting to know all of Hannah's secrets to make this whole college thing seem so effortless.

Hannah shrugged. "You really don't know anyone here?" she asked. I shook my head. "Damn, you're like a lost little bird. Don't worry, Cav, I may be from Green Bay, but Chicago is *my* town. Most of my friends graduated before me and moved out here. Some are at Loyola, some at UChicago, but I'm the only one from the basketball team that came to the artsy school. Tara is a junior at Loyola, interns at the Tribune, and she's having a thing tonight at her place, supposed to be a bunch of people there. Tara's a cool chick. We dated for a few months when she first moved out here, but don't worry, it was a chill breakup, and we're cool now, but I'd feel less weird if I showed up with someone tonight, so whaddya say?"

"Oh!" I exclaimed, embarrassed at how surprised I sounded. "So you're, I mean, you're a… I mean, I'm not … ugh, sorry. Yeah, cool, yeah, sure."

Hannah laughed so hard she had to wipe tears from her eyes. "How small *is* that town you're from?"

"Small," I said, feeling my face get hotter by the second. "Sorry," I stammered. "I promise I'm really progressive." I rolled my eyes. "God, I sound like such an idiot right now."

Hannah caught her breath from laughing. "It's been a while since I shocked someone by liking girls."

"I'm not shocked," I protested.

"It's fine, Cav. I'm bi. It's not a big deal. I'm guessing you're straight as hell, though, by your level of surprise."

"Yeah…" I said, unsure of what else to say.

"Right on. God makes all kinds! Am I right?" she said, fanning the polish on her fresh pedicure.

"Sure does," I said, wondering if I even believed in God anymore or if I ever had.

"I'm picking out your outfit, though," Hannah playfully demanded. "No goth boots in front of my crew."

"Deal," I said through a growing smile.

After a lot of sifting through my drawers and a lot of "you've got to be kidding me" glances, Hannah finally picked out some acceptable finds from my wardrobe: a red pencil skirt, a black sleeveless blouse, and some strappy sandals. I felt naked.

"I've never worn this skirt without leggings underneath it before," I said, shielding my pale legs from the mirror as I assessed my appearance. "Ugh, I have cankles. I hate my legs."

"Shut up," she snapped semi-playfully. "You're a rail. Deal with it."

"Thanks!" I said, unable to stop the grin from spreading over my face.

"Umm … that wasn't a compliment," she replied. "Too skinny."

Perfect, I thought, knowing she was wrong but satiated by every word.

Hannah was dressed in a gold crop top that exposed her perfect stomach that caved and curved in all the right places. Her black mini skirt and red pumps made her long legs longer, and she shook her hair out and tousled it so it would lay wild around her face. I would've died to know what it felt like to be that pretty.

"Up for a quick pre-game shot?" she asked, pulling a Grey Goose bottle from the mini-fridge in the corner. I let out an audible gasp.

"We can't have alcohol in here," I whispered.

"It's college, Cav. Vodka in the dorm fridge is practically a prerequisite." She poured two shots into mismatched shot glasses, downing the first one by herself and pouring another quickly, shoving the other in my direction. "Cheers. To a new … everything," she said, raising the glass above her head, waiting for me to do the same.

I was frozen, remembering the promise I had made to myself to not drink, to keep myself in control at all times. But suddenly, I felt every one of the 172 miles in between myself and Carter, Josh, and the cigarette-soaked diner. All of it was far, far away.

I took the shot glass from Hannah and, with my other hand, took my phone out of my purse and handed it to her.

"If I'm drinking tonight, you hold my phone. And don't let me near it even if I beg."

Hannah's lips pursed in a knowing smile, and she dropped my phone into her silver clutch, motioning me with her eyes to take the shot.

I closed my eyes and took a swig, the familiar burn creeping down my throat as I coughed, grabbing my nearby water bottle to rinse the taste of gasoline from my mouth. But I smiled when my stomach started to warm. I raised the empty shot glass toward Hannah's face.

"One more, roomie!" I shouted, not recognizing my own voice when it was tinged with joy.

I remember taking that shot and then maybe a couple more, but at some point between the dorm elevator and the party, everything went black.

****

The room was still spinning when my eyes finally peeled open, exposing the foggy and semi-familiar surroundings of my new dorm room.

"Ugh," I groaned, my mouth feeling like a mix of cotton and sand.

"There's water and Advil on your nightstand," I heard Hannah say from the other side of the room.

"Ugh," I said again, sitting halfway up in bed and grasping for the nearby cup, taking long, slow gulps as my head pounded. "What happened?" I rubbed my eyes.

"Not surprised you don't remember," Hannah said, walking toward me. I squinted to bring her into focus as she sat on the end of my bed. "You went too hard too fast, I guess. We weren't even at the party for an hour before I had to drag your ass home." She smiled.

"Noooo…" I droned, burying my head back into my pillow. "I made you leave?" I squeaked.

"I mean, you didn't *make* me do anything, but it became pretty clear that you needed to go home, so…"

"No, ugh, I'm so sorry," I said, unable to meet Hannah's gaze.

"It happens," she said. "Not the first time, not the last, right?"

Actually, yes, I'm hoping it will be the last, I thought, but "right" is what came out. I wasn't ready to let Hannah know that partying had not exactly been a frequent hobby of mine.

"Oh God," I said, sitting up sharply. "My phone…"

"You mean this phone?" Hannah waved my cell above her head. "It was in my purse all night."

"Thank you, thank you," I gushed, clutching the phone to my chest in gratitude before scrolling through my recent texts and calls to make sure nothing had been sent in the haze of last night. It hadn't, and I let out a deep sigh. "Wait, so, what happened? With … Kara?"

"Tara," she corrected me quickly. "Yeah, her new girlfriend was there, like basically everyone there was paired up. So I was fine making an early exit. You were a good excuse for that." She laughed.

"Did I do anything … embarrassing?" I asked through gritted teeth, unsure if I wanted to know the answer.

"I dunno, just typical drunk white girl shit, nothing crazy."

"Oh, okay, cool," I replied, having no idea what that meant but nodding in a knowing affirmation.

"Trust me, Cav, skinny white drunk college girls are kinda a dime a dozen, so I doubt anyone will even remember you."

"I've never been so relieved to be forgettable." I chuckled.

"Yeah, well, you owe me one, so next time *I* get to go hard, and *you* get to babysit, k?"

"Next time?" I said through a raised pitch of my increasingly hoarse voice.

"Yeah! Anyway, we're gonna be late for orientation," Hannah said as she stood up.

"Oh, right," I said, rubbing my eyes.

"And you look a little crazy, so ya may want to check a mirror before we head out," she offered as she began pulling clothes out of her dresser. "And, Cav, don't wear your goth boots to orientation. It's like a hundred degrees outside. Mkay?"

I nodded, putting my hands up to my pounding head. Getting out of bed felt like an impossible task. But then a sudden, unwelcome flash of Carter and Olivia's infamous beach photo entered my mind, and the adrenaline pushed me upright. *Maybe forgetting a whole night wasn't such a bad thing*, I thought, wishing it was that easy to forget so much more.

Chapter Ten

By the time classes had started the following week, I had mapped out exactly where to go on which days at which times. The specificity of my detailed schedule was comforting. I left my dorm much earlier than necessary to make it to my first class and still leave plenty of time if I got lost. The air was thick, muggy, and rich with distraction. The sound of car horns and conversation was so rife with energy that it began to just all blend into one perfect hum that never got old. My eyes craned upward to the tall cement structures as I meandered, squeezing by dozens of fast-paced power walkers on their way to the next essential item on their to-do list.

I longed to be like them, so jaded by the cityscape and bustle that it felt normal to careen between buildings and snake through lines of cars stuck in stand-still traffic. These Chicagoans were attentive, driven, and focused only on what was next. The businesswomen wore designer suits and tennis shoes with red-soled pumps peeking out of their snakeskin purses. The young professionals video chatted with friends and colleagues as they walked briskly toward their modern offices. But I couldn't take my eyes off the skyline, stopping to read every placard sign and trace my fingers over the gold engraved numbers on the sides of buildings.

I was one of them now, technically, but couldn't shake the Oakwood from my shell-shocked stares. Everything was different, from the streets themselves to the people who stood atop them. Instead of flat grassy sprawls of single-level homes, vertical stretches of cement reached toward the clouds. I was hooked.

When I finally found myself in front of the

building where my first class was, I pushed open the heavy glass door of the tall, mirrored entryway to see what looked like hundreds of other students milling about the chic, vast lobby. They were gathering around the directory in the center that listed room numbers and class names. I quietly pushed myself to the middle of the herd and squinted until I saw Communications 101 was on the third floor.

There were a few other students strewn around the room and one tall twenty-something woman writing on the whiteboard as she waited for the room to fill up.

"Hi, I'm Andrea Cavanaugh," I said to the woman. "Which seat is mine?"

She stopped writing and turned to face me with a knowing smile as she stifled a small laugh.

"Uh, wherever," she said before turning back around.

"Are you, um, Professor ... Santiago?" I asked, scrolling through the notes on my phone.

"No, I'm his grad assistant. He's on his way. Just sit wherever, okay?"

I nodded and found a seat a few rows from the back. I sat down gingerly and took some things out of my backpack, placing them neatly on the desk: my freshly charged laptop, a small notebook, a leopard-print mechanical pencil, and an unopened bottle of sparkling water.

I studied the other students methodically as they trickled in, some slouching in their chairs and some perked upright, some eagerly typing notes while others sat back and nodded. Professor Santiago finally walked in, loosening his mauve scarf and shuffling through some papers in his briefcase. He was a small man with round, magnified glasses that made his caramel eyes look twice as big as they really were. He had a short, white beard and wore a sweater vest and linen scarf despite the sweltering humidity outside. I barely remember the lecture as I just couldn't stop drinking in my surroundings.

I knew the answers to all of the questions he posed to the class since I'd done all the suggested pre-reading, but I never raised my hand. The students toward the front seemed to feed off the validation of being right, so I let them.

"Hey, can I borrow a pen? My tablet died," a low voice from behind me whispered in my direction. I turned to face the voice and felt my heart stop when I saw a mess of unkempt, curly brown hair atop the faceless co-ed. It wasn't Josh, but this stranger's hair was so similar that I sat frozen as my stomach churned with acidic nausea.

"It's okay if you don't have one. I can ask someone else," the man said quietly as I stared at him in awkward horror.

Without speaking, I grabbed a pen from my bag and tossed it on his desk, swinging back in my chair to face the front, feeling my pulse race to catch up as my breathing shallowed.

Grey laptop. Brown desk. Black pen, I repeated in my head.

Grey laptop. It's not Josh. Brown desk. He's not here. Black pen. I'm okay.

As the class ended, I shoved the contents of my desk back into my bag and flung out of the room, pushing past a few others to get outside where I could find air.

The beautiful, distracting hum from the city enveloped me once again and pushed every strand of those unkempt brown curls out of my mind. I paused against the side of the building until my breathing steadied enough for me to plunge back into the crowd, letting the humming current carry me upstream to find my next class.

****

Walking back to my dorm after the first full day of school, I had been to three classes in three different buildings and already had two reading assignments due next week. I was feeling a mix of harrowingly overwhelmed and eerily confident. It sent a thrill through my body to be amidst a city that felt so alive. Here I was just one of many and could achieve the anonymity I'd so craved. In Oakwood, someone like Carter was this rare endangered species, a mix of beauty and talent and mystery, but they were everywhere in Chicago. I tripped over brooding artists with smoldering eyes on every pathway through campus. I told myself that even Carter Wells was just one of many, too, and tried really, really hard to believe it whenever flickers of his half-smile flashed through my mind. But I hadn't reached out to him, which I felt proud of, though I couldn't help but wonder if he'd noticed.

So much of my time was spent trying not to think about Carter, but whenever the pit of loneliness in my stomach threatened to surface, I did my best to shove it back down and stay distracted. It was getting harder to ignore, though. Every morning I'd grab my phone to look for a new text. "Hey, babe," it would say in my mind. "Let's meet for breakfast before your first class." But the text never came. Carter was not here. The man who gracefully belonged to nobody yet somehow belonged to everybody, just not me, just not now.

"Hey, stranger." Hannah skipped over from across the way. "How was your day?" Her navy-blue backpack bounced against her assertive stroll as she caught up to me.

"Good, I guess. Just a lot to take in. How are you so peppy? I didn't even see you come home last night?"

"Yeah, it got crazy over at Ramy's party. I just stayed the night. You were gone when I came back to get ready."

"Ramy?" I asked. "No, but really, you've been out like every night since we got here. How do you have this much energy?"

"I dunno, just a lot of practice, I guess." She smiled wide. "Yeah, Ramy is a friend of a friend who lives on the other side of campus. It was that nineties-themed party, remember? You should've come. It was awesome."

"Yeah, but we had class today, and after last time, I couldn't imagine trying to go to class all hungover."

"Well, you don't have to drink until you blackout, ya know." She giggled.

"Well, yeah…" I trailed off. Hannah looked rested, energized, and fresh, hardly like someone who'd been out every night.

"Well, *my* first day of classes went great, thanks for asking," she said pointedly.

"Oh, right. Well, that's good," I replied.

"I'm gonna go change and work out. Wanna join me?"

"That's a hard pass," I said, itching to start my reading assignments and scour the Internet while pretending I wasn't trying to stumble upon what Carter had been up to.

"Suit yourself. Hey, did you call that guy yet about that job?"

"Jake? No, I was gonna call him this week," I said. I'd told Hannah that Jake was *my* family friend, conveniently leaving Carter's name out of the story, and that he might be able to hook me up with a hostess job or something at his pub, Blush, near campus. I wasn't sure what, if anything, Carter had told him about the sudden change of plans, but I figured it couldn't hurt to ask Jake if he was still hiring.

I needed something to do with my evenings that didn't involve Internet stalking my exes, self-pity, or blacking out; plus, not having to continually ask my parents for spending money sounded really appealing. I had worked part time during high school at the Oakwood Country Club, serving soft drinks and snacks to rich golfers who tipped well and smelled like cigars. It wasn't hard and the pay was decent, despite the long summertime, but now I hoped that having some customer service experience could help me land a trendier restaurant job in the city.

"Cool, I'm gonna see if the gym on campus is hiring when I head over there today. Want me to get you an application?" she asked.

"No thanks, that's not really my scene."

"Oh, okay, so it's like that? We have one day of college, and we're already snobs?" Hannah joked. "I see how it is."

"No, I just mean, look at you. You're like a fitness model, so it makes sense, but I'm ... well, *less* like that." I laughed, gesturing toward my black skirt, studded belt, and Jack's Mannequin t-shirt.

"Hmm, yeah, I guess you'd have to trade the goth boots for some tennis shoes." She tried to keep a straight face, but we both laughed.

Later that evening, I changed into some neutral brown pants, a floral blouse, and dressy sandals to walk to Blush and beg for a job despite my lack of Carter in tow. As I followed the directions on my phone, it started vibrating as my parents' picture popped onto the screen. I stopped walking and answered.

"Andrea! How are you?" My mom's bright voice made me feel instantly warm.

"Hi, Mom," I replied. "I'm actually on my way somewhere. Can I call you later?"

"Sure, I just wanted to check in. How was the big first day?"

"Yeah, I'm good. Classes were okay. I like my journalism professor, I think."

"That's great, hon. Did you find everything okay?"

"Yep, all good."

"Great. And have you stopped by the health center yet to sign up for therapy?"

"Mom…"

"Don't get a tone. You know that's important."

"Yes, I start next week." The lie tasted bitter in my mouth, but I didn't pull it back.

"Oh, that's great!"

"Mmhmm," was all I could get out, the guilt seeping from my voice. "I gotta go, Mom, sorry. I'll call you later or tomorrow before class, okay? Love you."

"Okay, love you, too. Miss y—"

I hung up quickly and took a deep breath, re-opening my maps app. Blush was only a ten-minute walk from my dorm.

I'll go to the health center tomorrow, I told myself. It felt better to pretend.

As I walked, I tried to push all the Oakwood out of my mind and immerse myself back into the Chicago hum. When I finally got to Blush, the pink hue from the cursive neon sign above the door told me I had made it.

If I tap my left hand on my leg and then my right hand and then tap both my feet twice, I will get the job, I told myself, obeying the ritual and inhaling a faux confidence that gave me just enough energy to push open the front door. It was only seven PM on a Monday, but the front lobby looked like midnight on New Year's Eve, dark and airy with twinkling fuchsia lights sprinkled throughout and bottles of sparkling wine with pastel labels posed in silver backlit cases. There was a large host desk at the end of the long front hallway draped in black velvet with a slender young woman sporting an angular blonde bob and bold red lipstick standing behind it.

"Table for ... one?" she asked dryly.

"No, uh, I'm looking for Jake?" I asked timidly, my eyes drinking in the lush atmosphere.

The blonde woman picked up a phone, pressing a single button. "Jake? Someone's here for you." She put her palm over the receiver and looked at me. "What's your name?"

"Andrea. Andrea Cavanaugh. I'm a ... a friend of Carter Wells."

"Andrea, something... Carter Wells... Okay, I'll tell her, thanks." She hung up. "Jake will be out in a moment." She refocused her attention on the couple behind me, quickly escorting them toward the back of the restaurant, where I heard some acoustic music, a woman's voice echoing Tom Petty covers over her guitar. As I craned my neck to catch a glimpse, I heard my name over the noise.

"Andrea," a man bellowed. I turned around to see Jake, a hefty middle-aged man with a thick beard, bushy brown hair, and kind eyes.

"Me. That's me!" I said, bouncing toward him. "Jake?" I extended my hand to shake his.

"Apologies, but have we met?" he asked, raising his thick eyebrow.

"No, sorry, maybe I should've called. I'm a friend of Carter Wells."

"Yeah, I was surprised to hear Janine say his name. I haven't heard from that guy in years, probably not since I moved to Chicago. Is he okay?"

"Yes," I said plainly. "I'm sorry, Jake, there must be a misunderstanding. Carter had talked to you about a job here, at Blush, bartending, I think. He was supposed to move here last week, with me, but he... Well, there was a change of plans, and now it's just me, and I'm only eighteen, so I know I can't bartend, but I thought maybe if you had another opening I could, like, host or serve or whatever you need. I just—"

"Whoa, whoa, whoa," Jake said. "I'm sorry, Andrea, is it?" I nodded. "Andrea, I'm sorry, but I haven't heard from Carter in years. I don't know what he told you, but there's definitely no job waiting here for him. Nice kid. I used to live down the street from his family, and his old man was nice enough to let me spend holidays there sometimes after my divorce, but like I said, it's been years..."

"I'm sorry," I said, fighting back tears as my face flushed. "Of course he didn't call you. Typical. I'm sorry. I'm such an idiot." I started back toward the door.

"Hey, it's okay. Do you still want an application? We are actually hiring for a hostess. Janine's starting night classes next month, and we could use someone on a few evening shifts per week. It's just part time. I haven't even posted it yet, but hey, let's say as a favor to Carter's dad and his famous Christmas smoked ham, what the hell. If your application checks out, I'll call you."

"Oh my God, thank you, Jake, you won't regret it. I'm a really hard worker, and your place here is so cool, and I promise—"

"Okay, okay, just fill this out and leave it with Janine. I gotta get back to my office, but it was nice meeting you, Andrea. I'll see you around." He forced a smile and disappeared behind a dark curtain adorned with an EMPLOYEES ONLY sign.

The creeping sensation of betrayal was bubbling up my throat so much so that I could taste its familiar corrosive burn. But I could not think about Carter Wells at this moment. I pulled a pen from my purse and sat on one of the long, shiny black booths in the lobby, furiously filling out the application, my thoughts feeling less coherent by the moment.

"I haven't heard from that guy in years." Jake's words echoed through my body. I couldn't understand why Carter would lie to me about Jake, but still move forward with breaking up his band and filling my head with false promises if he'd seemingly never intended to move. Maybe he was just as confused as I was. I wanted so deeply to hate him. And at that moment, it felt almost possible as I choked back the tears I had grown so tired of.

When I finished the form, I left it at the desk and tried to smile at Janine. She took it from me slowly, a puzzled look on her face.

"You okay?"

"Mhm, that's for Jake. Please. Thank you," I muttered, turning away. The front hallway felt endless as my brisk walked turned into a slow jog until I burst through the doors, breathing in the warm city air and finally letting the tears fall as I balanced against the side of the stone building.

So stupid. So stupid. I am so stupid. He was never coming here. Of course he was never coming here. My thoughts raced. I took a deep, shaky breath and steadied my balance.

White sandals. Black pants. Grey sidewalk. I tried to pull myself into the present moment and calm my quickened breathing. *White sandals. Of course he left me.*

Black pants. Did he ever love me? Grey sidewalk. I will always just be Josh's ruined leftovers. White sandals. Black pants. Grey sidewalk. I'm in Chicago. Far away from Josh. Nobody here knows Josh. I am safe. The thoughts were coming faster than I could keep up with. And I hated how Josh's name always managed to get thrown into the mix during these moments of swelling panic. I couldn't even have a breakdown about a different boy without Josh forcing his way into my head.

My breathing calmed, and the tears stopped. I wiped my face with a crumpled tissue from my purse and started walking back toward my dorm. I thought about texting Stephanie or Ethan but quickly decided against it. Instead, I opened my phone and scrolled to the Instagram icon, deleting the app before I even had a chance to hesitate. There would be no more obsessing over Carter's whereabouts or wondering what color bikini Olivia Schroeder was wearing today. I hoped he was lying to her, too. And I hoped they'd both get hurt in the process, being miserable under their shiny hair and soft skin.

Chapter Eleven

When I got back to the dorm, I found Hannah at her desk, wearing big round glasses with a green highlighter in one hand and a pencil tucked messily into her tightly wound updo. She was wearing blue gym shorts and a baggy Nike t-shirt, the teal polish starting to chip on her toenails, and a big *Introduction to Architecture* textbook sprawled in front of her.

"And she's a good student, too," I moaned, flopping onto my bed. "Of course she is."

"Tell anyone, and I'll kill you," she joked.

"How do you do it all, Hannah? Study, workout, party, I don't get it."

"Work hard, play hard, girl. And nothing in between. That's my motto."

"Yeah."

"What's wrong? How'd it go at Blush?"

"Fine," I lied, not wanting to feel Carter's name in my mouth anymore today. "We'll see if I get the job." There was a long pause, so I sat up and looked at Hannah, who was still staring at me. "What?"

"Well, I got the job at the gym, thank you for asking," she said tensely.

"Oh, right. Cool. I'm happy for you."

"Yeah? Tell your face," she said, turning back to her book as she tucked one leg against her body while she highlighted.

Jake called the next day to offer me the part-time hostess job, which I happily accepted in a rushed, grateful flurry of words. I could picture him rolling his eyes on the other end of the call, but I squealed when I hung up. Being employed now made being in Chicago feel much more permanent, which I loved. When my start date arrived the following week, I practically skipped the whole way to Blush, ready for something new and distracting where I could turn off my brain and just follow directions amidst the black velvet and twinkly lights of the front lobby.

It took a while to learn my way around the restaurant, probably longer than Jake would've liked. Janine was less than patient when it came to training me, so I just tried to study her breezy interactions with customers and the detail-oriented manner in which she managed the reservation book. I stayed in the background and mimicked her behaviors when necessary.

"Nice to see you again, Mrs. Gibbard," I'd say when the kind old woman with striking white hair and expensive jewelry came in for her Friday evening martinis. "Welcome back, Dr. Cuomo," I'd croon to the dapper oncologist who showed up every weekend to dine with a woman who looked half his age. "Have a good night, girls!" I'd shout to the bachelorette party who stumbled into the night air through fits of obnoxious laughter.

I was good with the customers, and it was easy to be. I could just tell how each one wanted to be talked to. I'd raise an eyebrow and fake a gasp when Mrs. Gibbard's bridge club crowd told me about how someone's granddaughter had a baby out of wedlock. I'd shine a flirtatious smile when I seated Dr. Cuomo since he clearly appreciated being fawned over by young women. But it wasn't as easy to figure out my co-workers.

For the most part, I stayed pretty invisible, but once in a while, a server would bark frustration toward me if I sat too many people in their section at once or not enough. It was a balance I tried obsessively to meet so I could avoid the raised voices that made me cower. If I looked to Janine for backup, she'd just shrug her shoulders and leave me to stumble through an apology while the servers scoffed and made a backhanded comment about my age. So I tried to analyze the preferences of each colleague and oblige their individual quirks.

After I was deemed no longer a "trainee," Janine transitioned to the day shift, and I was left to fend for myself against the sharp-tongued waitstaff. But even so, I was really just grateful to be somewhere that wasn't school, where my brain was constantly running, or the dorm—where I was getting used to dodging Hannah's questions about my past with vague, brush-off answers. At Blush, nobody asked questions. The work was easy enough, and there was no fear of running into someone I didn't want to see. So, despite the snippy attitudes, it was kinda like heaven.

One night during closing, I saw a group of servers talking and laughing together as they walked toward the front and then suddenly get quiet.

"Oh, come on, just invite her," one of them said.

I felt my face burn. Maybe I wasn't as invisible as I'd thought. I kept my head down as I pretended to be busy looking in the reservation book.

"She's like twelve," someone responded quietly.

"Don't be a dick, just invite her."

I wanted to crawl under the desk as I heard footsteps approach me.

"Hey, new girl," a woman said.

I looked up to see Sarah, a curvy redhead with heavy makeup who I hadn't officially met yet but had enjoyed watching interact with the customers. She always laughed loudly at the men's jokes and complimented the women's outfits. I bet she got great tips.

"Hi," I replied nervously.

"The Blush crew is coming to my place tonight. You in?"

"Oh, that's okay," I said, thinking that was the answer she wanted to hear.

"Oh, come on, Andrea," a man echoed from the group behind Sarah. I didn't think anybody there knew my name.

"Dean, she said no," Sarah snapped.

"She's just nervous. It's okay. We don't bite." Dean was a bartender and probably in his mid-thirties, I guessed. He had short, thick brown hair with a few visibly grey strands, prominent eyebrows, and dark, rugged stubble. His t-shirts were always too tight, but that complemented his hefty, strong arms, which I guessed was the point. He had olive-toned skin, a small scar above his lip, and a gruff voice that always sounded both tired and irritated. I'd never seen him smile. Hearing my name come from his mouth sounded unnatural.

"I know…" I stammered.

"Great. Give Sarah your number, and she'll text you her address." He pulled on a worn leather jacket as the group continued toward the door. Sarah rolled her honey-colored eyes and thrust her phone toward me. I quickly tapped my number onto her keypad and handed it back.

"See you later, I guess," she said flatly before jogging to catch up with the others who were already outside. Bewildered, I grabbed my phone and texted Hannah.

Me: **Something weird just happened.**
Hannah: **What?**
Me: **My co-workers just invited me to hang out.**

Hannah: **So?**

Me: **Idk, I think they're a lot older. And I think it's a party?**

Hannah: **What time are we going?**

Me: **Lol, seriously?**

Hannah: **Swing by and get me on your way.**

Me: **I didn't say I was going.**

Hannah: **See you soon!**

I grabbed my purse and walked out into the warm, wispy night air. I couldn't shake this nagging in my gut that said to just go home and go to bed, but that's what Oakwood Andrea would've done, the boring Andie who had two friends and lived vicariously through their escapades on Instagram. I left that Andie in Michigan where she belonged. Maybe now I could grow into the girl that Hannah thought she knew, the one who'd partied too hard the first night, had a mysterious past, and worked at a trendy pub.

By the time I got to the dorm, Hannah was waiting outside, waving enthusiastically when she saw me.

"All right, where are we going?" she chirped, flashing a peek of the rhinestone-encrusted flask from her purse, a broad smile across her face.

"I just want to go inside and change first," I noted as I pushed the front doors open to our building.

"Aw, boo, fine. Wait, will you *finally* let me do your makeup?" Hannah asked excitedly.

I nodded. "I think it's time to make some changes."

"Oh, thank *God*," Hannah exclaimed as we reached our room. I threw my purse on the bed and sat down at her desk.

"Try and make me look ... well, like you." I laughed. "Or just ... not like me at least."

Hannah threw me a makeup removing wipe, and I patted it over my face, watching the residue from my signature smoky eyeliner flake onto the wipe.

"I just think you need something a little brighter, maybe," Hannah offered as she dug through her kit of eye pencils and highlighters. "Like here, this velvet ruby color will kill on your big lips." She shoved a gold tube of lipstick in front of me. "First, put on your own concealer, and then come back and I'll have some eye stuff picked out." I obliged.

"I'm just gonna put my hair up tonight," I said. I had let the siren-red highlights fade from my sandy hair for the first time in years. "I found a new hairstyle online that I really want to get." I opened the photo on my phone and showed Hannah.

"Cute. Yeah, that'd look good on you," she replied.

The model in the picture stared back at me, daring me to try to look like her. She had flawless champagne-hued locks with side-swept bangs that were both delicate and sexy. I was planning on spending my entire first paycheck on this new haircut and color next week.

"With this red lipstick and a pushup bra, nobody is gonna notice your faded hair tonight. Promise." Hannah lined up her selections for me on the desk. "Okay, Cav, ready when you are."

I finished dabbing my foundation against my cheeks and sat by Hannah, closing my eyes as she swept pastels against my skin until she held up a mirror in front of me, admiring her work.

"Thank you!" I gushed. "I look different. It's perfect."

"Great!" she said proudly. "Now change into something a little softer, like maybe a cami, skinny jeans, and some strappy wedges? And, yes, you can borrow my strappy wedges." She laughed. I nodded and started pulling things from my closet. "And don't smudge my masterpiece," she reminded, gesturing to my face. "Where is this party tonight anyway?"

"It's an apartment that looks, like, maybe a fifteen-minute walk away?" I guessed, showing her the map from my phone screen where I'd typed Sarah's address.

"Perfect. So, who's all going to be there? What're they like?" she asked as I pulled on the new clothes.

"Umm, honestly, I barely know these people. Tonight was the first real conversation we've had. I think they only invited me out of pity."

"Well, a pity date is better than no date," Hannah declared, taking a quick sip from her flask and tucking it safely back into her purse.

"Is it?"

"Sure! Okay, ready to go? You look fab."

"Thanks! And yes, let's go," I replied as we started toward the door and back into the night air that was growing brisker each day.

"So, who should I pay attention to tonight? Anyone cute?"

"I don't know, not really. They're kinda ... old?"

"Old like thirty? Or old like fifty?"

"More like thirty."

"Phew, Cav, don't scare me like that. So, whatever, we'll be like a breath of fresh air to them, then. I mean, they work at Blush. It's not like they're some stuffy executives that're gonna sip wine and talk about their investment plans. We'll be fine."

"I guess," I said, trying to force the nagging discomfort in my stomach to venture back down to a more manageable whir I could ignore.

****

My hands started shaking as we walked up the steep, creaky staircase to Sarah's apartment. When we finally reached the right floor, Hannah stopped me in the dim hallway.

"You've been kinda quiet. You okay?" she asked sincerely, scanning my face for answers.

"Yeah, sorry, I guess it's just, like, I work with these people, so I don't want to embarrass myself."

"Cav, I got you. Just chill. Be yourself."

Yeah, right, I thought. *That's what I'm worried about.* I clenched my fists to stop from trembling. I couldn't even understand exactly what I was scared of. It was just this nauseating wave of unease—but I couldn't succumb to that here, not in this dingy apartment building with peeling wallpaper and flickering hall lights. Hannah pulled the glittery flask from her purse and shoved it toward me.

"This will help," she offered. "Just pace yourself this time."

I gladly accepted, taking a gulp of some kind of clear, pungent alcohol that burned my throat and warmed my chest, pushing some of the darkness to the side as it spread through my veins. I nodded as we ventured to Sarah's door, which was already open a crack. Hannah pushed it further, exposing a large room with old, mismatched furniture and about a dozen of my co-workers in different pockets of the space, all briefly turning to look as we entered before quickly re-engaging in their prior conversations.

"Hey, whaddya got to drink here?" Hannah brazenly asked the first person she saw, a trendy busboy with a handlebar mustache who pointed her toward the tiny kitchen where there was an array of liquor, beer, and mixer bottles strewn atop the messy counter. "Thanks!

Come on, Cav." She tugged my arm and pulled me toward the drinks, pouring a generous amount of vodka and splash of seltzer into two plastic cups. It felt better to have something to hold while I studied the room.

"You showed," Dean said from behind us. His deep voice startled me as it echoed over the bustle of the room.

"And who is this?" Hannah asked loudly, gesturing to Dean with a knowing giggle that reminded me just how eighteen we were. I took a sip of my drink, tensing as the cheap, dry liquor both soothed and shocked my tongue.

"Dean," I choked. "That's Dean. And that's Hannah."

"Nice to meet you, Dean," Hannah buzzed.

"Pleasure," he replied. Hannah's leggy, athletic stature and four-inch heels towered over Dean, making him look suddenly smaller and thicker than I'd remembered. He'd slicked his hair back since I'd last seen him. "What're you ladies drinking?"

"Oh, whatever I found over there. We're not picky," Hannah said.

I finally saw Sarah from the other side of the room and tried to wave softly. She laughed when she saw Dean talking to us, pointing it out to the girls she was talking to.

"Oh," I said, surprised. "Apparently, someone's not happy to see me."

"Sarah? Ignore her. Trust me, she just wishes she was your age." He laughed. "Let me guess … twenty?"

"Eighteen." I blushed. Dean's eyebrows raised.

"Very cool," he crooned, stepping closer to me, a fog of sharp, minty cologne surrounding him.

"I'm gonna go mingle, Cav. Have fun," Hannah said excitedly, flashing me a thumbs-up as she backed away. I shot her a worried glare, but she had already turned away. Before I knew it, Dean's hand was slipped around my waist.

"Cav? Cute nickname. What's it from?" he asked quietly. His breath smelled like a mix of mouthwash and whiskey. I stood frozen, unsure if I wanted to run away or have him touch me, and feeling helplessly stuck in the gray of those two scenarios.

"Cav-Cavanaugh. Is my last name," I stammered, his hand tightening around my waist. I knew that however I reacted at this moment would be my answer to his puzzling advance. So I had to think carefully and quickly, but the rush from the vodka and warmth of his strong hand extending around my flinching waist was clouding any logical thoughts that attempted to surface. I quickly forgot any note I'd ever taken on flirting or just basic normal reactions amongst human beings in society. So I just stood there stiffly, letting him assume that my sheer lack of response was the same thing as a glowing approval.

I'd never considered Dean as attractive or unattractive before. I'd just really never considered Dean, period. My mind was usually consumed with school or Carter or whatever I could grab to distract myself from an impending flashback or swell of panic. This was new. I hadn't carved out space for it yet.

Dean grazed his hand under the back of my shirt just enough to send a sizzle through my spine. I exhaled quietly and deeply as his face moved closer to mine, the sharp prickles from his stubbled chin scratching my jawline as he began to softly kiss my neck, his hand tucking my hair behind my ear. His lips were chapped and determined.

Is this what adults do? Just say like three sentences to each other and then make out? Do I react or just let him go? Does he want me to react? Are people watching? Is this why he invited me? How old is he? Does it matter? My mind raced as my skin tingled. Before I could answer any of my own thoughts, he plunged his lips onto mine, starkly different than the gentle caressing I was used to from Carter's wide, aching kisses. I suddenly missed Carter so much that it hurt. I wondered if Olivia knew how Carter's mouth felt, fervent, and breathless. I shut my eyes tightly to keep from crying and kissed Dean back, letting him swallow me.

After a few minutes, I finally pulled back to breathe. Carter was no longer the last person I had kissed. And I hated everything about that.

"Want to go to the bedroom?" Dean asked quietly.

"Whoa, what?" I gasped.

"Well?" He bit his lip as he waited for my answer. My heart sank into that familiar, threatening pit that had seemingly burrowed itself permanently in my core. There was nothing beautiful about this moment. There was no lightning in this drafty apartment. Even the butterflies had turned to ash. The dark shadows I'd seen from Josh weren't here either, though. I guess this is what lived in between, just stale air soaked in cheap vodka that drifted between the beckoning bartender and me. Maybe this was what the world looked like in the gray between Carter and Josh, and if so, maybe I had to adapt. But I knew what "going to the bedroom" meant, and I didn't feel ready for that. Not with Dean. Maybe not with anyone, at least for a while.

"I-I don't know." I couldn't find my words.

"Come on, Cav, aren't we having a good time?" My new nickname sounded exactly right in this moment. I was far from Andie.

"I don't know," I said again.

"Ugh, Sarah was right." Dean sighed, letting his arms fall at his sides. "This was a mistake. You're just a kid."

"Whoa," I replied sharply. "I just said 'I don't know.'"

"Exactly," he snapped. "I need a drink." He pushed past me. Seeing the opening, Hannah bounced over, her eyes sparkling with excitement.

"Holy shit, I didn't know you had it in you! We were barely here two seconds, and you're making out with some guy!" she whispered happily, quickly changing her tone once she sensed my frozen despair. "What happened? What'd he do?" Her gaze darted around the room.

"No, nothing, it's fine. I just, I don't know if I like him. And I think he wants to … ya know…"

"And…?" Hannah seemed confused. "You don't have to profess your love for each other to just have some fun. You know that, right?" I nodded. "Look, that guy's hot and probably good in bed. You've been working so hard with school and everything. You deserve some fun. You're single, and you're young. It's not gonna be like this forever, so make the most of it. Live a little!"

I nodded again, taking a long, slow sip of my drink, injecting courage with each gulp. At some point after that, I left my body, but not in a dreamy, watching-myself-from-above kind of way. It was like I fell out of my skin, unable to control my movements and watching helplessly as a stranger in my clothes marched back to Dean, tapped his shoulder, and kissed him firmly on his dry, eager lips.

"Looks like someone changed their mind," he murmured.

I watched myself nod and be led into the bedroom, where he quickly unbuckled his belt, grabbed a condom from his pocket, bent me over an unmade bed atop a strewn floral comforter, pulled my panties aside, and shoved into me. I don't remember what it felt like. I don't remember if I said anything. I don't remember if I liked it. I just remember how heavy his sweaty, muscular body was as it stuck to my back. I remember his scratchy chin itching my shoulders from behind. And I remember afterward him slicking his hair back with his hands from where it had fallen into his face.

I entered my body again then after I was put back together, studying his blank expression as he fussed with his hair in the dresser mirror. It looked better when it was tousled in his eyes, but he seemed insistent on taming it back, scraping his fingernails against his scalp as he focused. It could've been five minutes or five hours since we entered the bedroom, but stumbling out again, I was lost. Dean had disappeared into the kitchen. I dove for Hannah, who was talking to a small group of loud hipsters in floppy hats. At some point, we left. I vaguely remember Dean winking at me as I walked out the front door, which made my stomach both flip and churn.

When the warm night air hit my face, it was as if Carter and the lightning had all vanished from my body, scattered throughout that dreary apartment, scrubbed from my ribs, leaving something deep and empty behind. Andie was gone now. I had intended to leave the part of me in Oakwood that was the pathetic shell that Josh hurt and Carter left, but somehow I had forgotten to keep the rest. Maybe there never was any more.

When I crawled into bed that night, the room felt still and silent; all the warmth had left my body. I lay there, unable to sleep as I begged my mind to send me memories of being wrapped in Carter's arms, safe in a fleeting moment, gracefully ignorant to his future intentions. But all that came were nightmares. I woke up with a gasp, my hands clammy with sweat.

"Who's Josh?" Hannah groaned from her side of the room.

"What?" I tried to steady my voice.

"This is like the third time I've woken up to you talking in your sleep about someone named Josh."

"Nothing. Nobody. Go back to sleep."

I heard Hannah sigh as she turned over in her bed, and I fell back into my pillow, afraid to close my eyes again. So I didn't. I grabbed my phone, hoping the pixelated screen would provide some distraction. A sting ran through my stomach when I saw a text from Dean. I'd forgotten that we'd exchanged numbers before my shameful stumble out of Sarah's bedroom.

Dean: **Fun night...**

Those dots could've meant anything, from sarcasm to mystery to flirting. I hated those three dots. But a new sensation started rolling through my body, like a glimmer that filled my lungs with a sudden burst of pure oxygen. I brazenly tapped a response, hitting send before I had a chance to reconsider.

Me: **Really fun! Let's do it again soon.**

No part of my body craved Dean's skin against mine again. My jawline was still raw from the scrape of his stubble. But this older guy, this *man*, apparently found me sexy, even "fun," and that was irresistible all on its own, even if Dean wasn't. I was invigorated, powerful. And I needed more.

When I didn't hear back from him, I decided to double down and try again to coax a response that might give me another shot of this new, exciting energy I was suddenly desperate for.

Me: **Hope you had a good rest of your night!**

See you at work tomorrow!

    Dean: **Thx...**

    The three dots again. God, how I hated those dots. But after minutes of focused analysis, I concluded that it was just Dean's way of being coy. Maybe I could grow to like those stupid dots.

Chapter Twelve

When the sun began to peek through the blinds the next morning, I set my phone down and sat up to quietly maneuver out of bed without waking up Hannah. Looking in the mirror, my eyes were dark, exhausted, and caked with last night's mascara. My head pounded, and my stomach growled. I tied my greasy hair into a bun and threw on some sweats from the floor of my closet. I saw a glass of water on my bedside table with two Advil and graciously guzzled it down, making a mental note to thank Hannah later.

I grabbed my laptop and some makeup remover wipes and stopped in the bathroom to collect myself before heading downstairs to the communal study where I could get some reading done before my classes started that day. But I kept rereading the same page before I realized I hadn't actually been reading anything at all. My mind kept drifting to my phone and those three dots. The hunger in my gut had turned to fluttery pangs when I thought about someone wanting me so badly last night that they had to crawl inside my body. But then it quickly switched to nausea when I thought about that someone being Dean. But maybe if I closed my eyes and focused *just* on the intoxicating desire, not the rough execution, I could keep floating for a while before some kind of inevitable crash.

Dean *was* cute in a dark, brooding, older man kinda way. And if he saw something in me that brought out this raw, animalistic attraction, maybe that would be enough, for a while at least. Maybe I could grow to meet him there and return the same fervor. Being devoured in lust for a night felt better than aching for Carter with every inch of my body, so I told myself this was the right next step.

I shuffled to class in a hazy emotional hangover and a cloud of floral body spray that I hoped masked the shower I hadn't taken yet. I looked straight ahead as I walked, having flashes of memory from last night flood my brain in bursts as I put one foot in front of the other. I only looked up once to see the Sears Tower glimmer against the sky, but the sunlight seared into my weary eyes, so I shielded them with my hand and pressed forward.

I piled into class toward the back of the herd, flopping onto a chair by the door. I wasn't sure I had the stamina to sit through the whole lecture.

When Professor Santiago began speaking, I settled deep into my oversized sweater, resting my head against my soft arm.

"Who can tell me what the transmission of messages without considering consequences is called?" he asked.

Disinhibition, I thought.

"Disinhibition," stated the perky brunette from the front row without raising her hand.

"Good, Rachel," the professor offered. "Can someone give me an example of disinhibition?"

Texting Carter that I miss him. Texting Josh that I hate him. Texting Dean that I want to see him again.

"Like, if someone forwards an inappropriate joke from a friend to a big group of colleagues, right?" Rachel said.

"Right, that's one example. Anyone else?"

The pounding in my head had returned, and the room felt like it was getting smaller by the minute. So I slithered out of my chair and through the back door, closing it quietly behind me and taking sharp breaths as soon as I was able to burst out of the building. I put my hand to my aching head and welcomed the distracting city hum as it swirled around me.

I stopped at the coffee shop on the corner by my dorm on the way home and downed a double espresso. It tasted terrible—I hated the earthy, sour flavor of coffee—but it had become necessary to survive the days when the nights offered such little sleep. I took a swig of diet soda to cleanse my palette and heard my phone vibrate against my bag.

Pulling it out, I saw Stephanie was calling on FaceTime. I grimaced when I thought about how long it had been since I talked to her. I seriously considered declining the call, but staring back at me was the picture I'd assigned to her contact years ago; it was a photo of us laughing over fruit smoothies at the mall during a break from prom dress shopping. She'd been invited by a senior that year, and the excitement was gushing from her eyes in the photo. We always looked so opposite, she in her pastel boho skirts and me in my edgy, dark denim. But there was a time in early elementary school where I can remember us looking exactly the same, from the awkward bangs to our matching rainbow leggings. And as the years ticked by and my style gradually shifted to hair dye and alternative band tees, she was the only constant I kept with me from the early days.

I eventually got into music and met Ethan, who shared my newfound love of dark humor and indie rock, while Stephanie fell into her own crowd mixed with smart upperclassmen who grew up fast and talked about politics. It got harder to stay in close touch as our lives began to untangle and stretch in different directions, but I never stopped cherishing her and what she'd meant to my life. I had just stopped telling her.

I reluctantly swiped open my phone and plastered the best version of a smile I could create.

"She's alive!" Stephanie sang from the other end.

"I'm alive!" I returned. "Sorry, I know it's been a while. I've been so busy."

"Sure, sure," she replied, smoothing her auburn hair with one hand as she walked. "Whatcha doin?"

"Just stopped in this coffee shop on my way back to the dorm."

"Fun. I'm heading into class soon but wanted to see if I could catch you first. Honestly, I'm kinda shocked you picked up!"

"Well, I miss you," I said sheepishly. "I'll call more, okay? I know we have a lot to catch up on."

"Yes, like this dorm you speak of ... pictures, please? And what's the roommate like? Have you met any boys? How're the classes?"

"Oh, um, she's chill. Kinda met a boy, but it's a long story. And classes are fine."

"Okay, Andie, you're not giving me much to work with here."

"Sorry, I'm just tired and have a lot on my mind."

"Well, I've got a few minutes until my class starts. What's up?"

"Nothing, sorry."

"Will you stop apologizing?"

"Sorry. I mean, yes."

"Okay, then! So, who's the boy?"

"Eh, it's really new. He's a bartender. But he's ... I don't know, he's older. I don't really want to talk about it yet."

"Okay," she said flatly. "Well, I'm doing great, thanks for asking," she finally stated after a long pause.

"Shit, sorry. I mean, ugh, of course I want to hear about how things are going with you. Do you like school?"

"Yeah, I mean, it's community college, so

nothing earth shattering, but I did join this really cool theater program that I'm pretty excited about."

"Yeah? That's awesome. I bet you're great in it. Hey, can I call you later? I'm almost back at the dorm and, like, desperately need a shower."

"Okay." Stephanie sighed. "Let's catch up soon, though, okay? For real."

"Yes, for real," I replied. "Thanks, Steph, love you, talk soon." I couldn't hang up fast enough. She always had a way of seeing right through me and finding the girl with awkward bangs and rainbow leggings still there somewhere behind all the eyeliner and apologies. I didn't want to feel seen in that moment. But I was ready to forget that girl existed so I could make way for something new, exotic, and lovable.

When I gratefully returned to the dorm, I stood under the hot shower faucet in my floor's communal bathroom for what felt like hours.

Wrapped in a cotton bathrobe and flip flops, I slipped back into my dorm room to find Hannah frantically pulling on clothes.

"I overslept!" she shouted. "I'm late for class."

"Can't you just skip it? Isn't this just your history lecture? All the notes are online. I just barely made it through the first half of comm today."

"Skip it and do what? Lay around here with you all day? No, I *can't* skip it. It's important. It's *all* important." She rushed her words as she hurriedly grabbed some tennis shoes from her closet.

"Geez, okay, whatever," I groaned. "I just mean, like, you don't *have* to do everything, Hannah. It's okay to give yourself a minute."

"You don't get it," she scoffed. "It's fine. I gotta go." She flung her bag across her shoulder and flew out the door.

"Jesus," I said out loud to no one, still whirling from the sudden encounter.

"Blue towel. Black flip flops. Pink loofah," I said, scanning my attire and shower caddy for items to ground me. *Blue towel. Black flip flops. Pink loofah.* I took a deep breath and stretched out on my bed, setting the alarm on my phone for an hour before my work shift started that evening in case I fell asleep. But the espresso and diet soda coursed through my veins, making rest an impractical task. Instead, I played in my mind what it would be like to see Dean at work that night. Would he greet me with a passionate embrace? Would he whisper something sexy to me in the break room? Did I want him to? I spent the next hour meticulously applying my makeup and curling the ends of my hair to mimic the effervescent way Olivia's locks flowed around her face in that beach photo that had been branded into my memory.

By the time my shift at Blush arrived, I had stopped in the bathroom before heading to the host stand so I could touch up any makeup that might have dissipated on my walk over. When I felt satisfied with my reflection, loving how little it resembled the Andie from Oakwood, I strode to the break room to punch in and put my purse away. Sarah was there getting ready for her shift, too.

"Hi, Sarah!" I surprised us both with my enthusiasm.

"Oh, hey," she said cautiously, fastening her black cloth apron around her wide hips.

"Have you seen Dean yet?" I chirped, excited to feel his eyes on me.

"Oh, sweetie," she said pitifully, holding back a laugh and avoiding eye contact.

"What?" I said, tilting my head and crossing my

arms tightly as I shifted my weight from one foot to the other.

Sarah sighed and rolled her eyes. "He's out back on a cigarette break."

"Thanks!" I stepped quickly through the kitchen to the back door, walking out into the alley lined with dumpsters and empty cardboard boxes.

I craned my neck to try to spot Dean amidst the garbage and other employees smoking or talking on their phones in between shifts. I finally recognized him from behind, so I walked quickly to greet him, buzzing off the anticipation of what he might say or do when he saw me. I pictured him being flooded with attraction and saying something hot that could keep me afloat for a while, drunk on appeal and illusion. But as I got closer, it became clear that he was not alone.

Dean was ravenously kissing a petite blonde waitress, pressing her against the brick wall of the alley, her neck bright red from his scratchy chin, his hips grinding into hers. They didn't look up as I approached. I put my hand over my mouth before I could let out a startled gasp and stumbled backward, quickly walking back into the restaurant, brushing past Sarah in the kitchen.

"Aww, did you find your boyfriend?" she snapped through a mocking giggle. I turned toward her, my face flush and eyes wet with insult. Her expression softened and she touched my arm, which I jerked away from her pale, freckled hand.

"Hon, come on. Sleeping with Dean is like a right of passage at Blush. I know you're young, which may be a new low for him if I'm being honest, but you can't take it seriously."

"I know!" I barked, turning and rushing to the host stand to start work, feeling every ounce of self-pity that burned through my skin as I greeted customers, convinced they all could read the pathetic story written across my face.

The hours crawled by painfully as I took notice of every minute that brought me closer to sprinting back to my dorm, where I could hide under blankets and books for the next four years. As I grabbed my purse from the break room, ignoring Sarah as she punched her timecard nearby, I felt a newly familiar hand graze my elbow.

"Hey, you," Dean said quietly, leaning against the wall.

"Hi." I stood stunned, frozen again in his confining presence.

"Done for the day?"

I nodded.

"Cool. Talk soon, yeah?" he asked, gazing at me through weary eyes.

I nodded again, and he squeezed my forearm before turning to walk out.

"That's mean, even for you, Dean. You're getting the poor girl's hopes up," Sarah sneered from behind us. Dean ignored her as he brushed by, running his hands through his dark hair as he left the room. I pretended not to hear her, too. The tingling intoxication was returning, and I didn't care about the blonde waitress anymore, or Sarah's quips, which I was now convinced were made out of jealousy, inadequacy, or both. I just wanted to protect this feeling and its intensity at all costs. The alternative was too dangerous.

Chapter Thirteen

As the warm, muggy air turned gradually into sharper, frosted breezes, I had begun mastering the art of building scar tissue around my heart. When Dean called, usually in the middle of the night, I'd bounce over to his studio apartment, groveling for touch and affirmation. And when he didn't call, when days and sometimes weeks of silence passed, I'd shield my eyes from the bar at Blush when I passed by. I told myself that the waiting just made it more exciting when he finally did respond, which he eventually always did. I tried not to think about what Dean did between our midnight encounters. I was happy not to ask, and I think he was happier not to answer.

My schoolwork was getting done, but often at the expense of sleep, which had become a rare luxury. My makeup was getting heavier to cover up the eyes that felt puffier by the hour, and my jeans were getting baggier as after-work cocktails often replaced standard sustenance. I looked less like Oakwood than I knew I could, and there was a rich, exhausting comfort in not recognizing myself.

As Thanksgiving neared, I toyed with the idea of going home for a long holiday weekend. I hadn't been back since moving to Chicago, and the thought of breathing in the slushy, sugary Oakwood air was nauseating. It had only been a few months, but the smoky dew of the big city clung to my skin, and I never wanted to wash it off. The idea of sitting in an Oakwood donut shop on Black Friday, being across the table from vague faces that only existed in the yearbook I'd shoved under my dorm-room bed, was too much.

I pictured myself wincing every time the door jingled, bracing my body for the panic that would come if I heard the sickeningly familiar swoosh of Josh's musty corduroys as he slinked into the room. Or running into Carter and feeling him look right past me as if he couldn't quite recall that girl he once pulled from darkness behind an old abandoned movie theater. It felt too fragile to test either scenario, so I'd been rehearsing lies about school or work to let my parents down easily. I couldn't go back, not yet. The skeletons I'd buried along the way weren't cold enough yet to take the risk of unearthing.

On a rare night off, I found myself alone in my dorm, itching with unease as my distractions had dwindled. Hannah was working. My homework was finished, and I felt the internal tug that came whenever I was alone and undisturbed. I knew the gentle nudge would soon turn into clawing desperation if I didn't feed it. So I texted Dean.

Me: **Hey, can I come over?**

I got up to rearrange my closet while I waited for his response, trying to keep my hands busy. I didn't really want to see Dean. It sounded exhausting to get ready, put on lacy underwear, and venture out in the cold just to scuff my new boots on the salted sidewalk and have a gruff bartender look straight through me for an hour. I didn't even have to fake the pleasure anymore—it was clear neither of us cared if I got off, just as long as he always did. For me, it was the intoxicating anticipation of feeling a man's hands against my skin that was worth every second.

Each time I went there, I knew I'd be stumbling out of his apartment sometime later with cigarette-scented hair, the stain of vodka and mouthwash still fresh on my tongue, and a spotty memory of our encounter, but I'd be too drunk on power to care. He'd wanted me, maybe briefly, maybe barely, but bad enough to get inside of my body. It didn't even matter if it felt good; being that powerful was like magic. When the loneliness was biting, I could cast this spell to feel luminary again, to become visible for a moment. It usually lasted a while, too, the afterglow, until I needed a recharge, but it had been weeks since I'd been to Dean's apartment, and the urge to feel needed had become incessant.

After ten grueling minutes, my phone finally chimed.

Dean: **Tonight's not good.**

I started a few different texts but erased each version before sending it. The first was too eager, the second too pleading, and the third was just pathetic. I'd learned that Dean never really changed his mind, so it saved me some mental gymnastics to just believe him the first time. But just because Dean was unavailable didn't mean my clawing solitude wouldn't bubble over tonight. I scanned through my contact list, hunting for a name that could tide me over until Dean was ready to make me feel a little more human again. Panic began to swell as I scrolled through names and numbers. I swallowed to try to keep it at bay, clenching my jaw to keep the bile at the base of my throat.

Nobody wants to hear from you. Nobody wants to touch you.

The thoughts were coming faster than I could digest.

Nobody wanted Andie then, and nobody wants Cav now.

My jaw trembled, and I swallowed again until I saw the name "Ethan Marks" staring back at me from the dimly lit screen.

Me: **I miss you.**

I sent the text before I could even consciously decide if it was a good idea or not. It was mere seconds until he started typing a response, and I couldn't help but analyze those three dots I'd grown to hate; this time, they flashed while Ethan responded.

I hadn't spoken to Ethan since I left. He had every right not to reply at all, but the flashing dots were a sweet reminder that he was still Ethan—forgiving, gentle Ethan. My mind began drifting to memories of lattes in the diner or sprawling out on the floor of my parents' basement while we shared a pair of headphones to listen to our favorite emo band that we didn't think our other friends were sophisticated enough to understand. I thought of the night after graduation, his drunk, wobbly voice begging me not to forget him. All I'd done since leaving was try. Before the guilt could seep too deeply into my veins, I let out an audible gasp of relief when his response came through.

Ethan: **What took you so long?**

Me: **I'm sorry.**

I meant it.

Ethan: **Coming home for Thanksgiving?**

Me: **I don't think so, busy at work and stuff.**

I didn't care that he knew I was lying.

Ethan: **Then I'm coming to Chicago. Next weekend?**

I bit my lip until it hurt and then bit a little harder until I winced and exhaled the pain. His insistence on seeing me felt good and warm and wove through my body more than the sensation of Dean's skin against mine ever could.

Black yoga pants. Grey walls. White pillow.

I began to come back into my body, landing safely on Ethan's affection.

Black yoga pants. Grey walls. White pillow. I'm in my dorm room. I am safe. Somebody wants to drive three hours just to see me. I'm okay.

I responded to Ethan as my eyes got heavy.

Me: **That's soon! I'm working until 10pm next Friday so maybe the following weekend?**

Ethan: **Next weekend is the only one without a Blank show until late December, so it's now or never!**

Ugh. I hated knowing that Intentionally Blank had gotten back together. It was just a sickening reminder that Carter was far from Chicago. I wondered if his bandmates or their fans cheered when they found out he left me and stayed in Oakwood, where they could keep playing at the same breweries and community theaters they'd performed at for years. I wondered if their first show without me was freeing for Carter. I wondered if he'd played the songs he wrote about me on stage or anywhere since the breakup. I wondered if Olivia knew who those songs were about. I tried to push these unwelcome thoughts aside and refocus on the parts of Ethan I'd loved long before he became Carter's drummer.

Me: **Okay, but only if you promise that we don't talk about/dwell on the past. I just want to have fun.**

Ethan: **See you next weekend!!**

I assumed that meant he agreed that there'd be no talk of Carter, Josh, or anything Oakwood. Maybe Ethan could cut it in my new world if he could leave those parts behind, too.

My eyelids started to drag as my weary body began to close into itself like a wilting flower. I crawled onto my bed, my stomach grumbling under the baggy sweatshirt. I tried to recall if I'd eaten dinner or not, but the welcome shelter of sleep enveloped me before I could even get under the covers.

Chapter Fourteen

A pang of nervous energy jolted through my chest when I got Ethan's text saying he'd arrived. It was late Friday night, and I'd just gotten back to the dorm after a six-hour shift at Blush.

"Slow down, girl," Hannah said from her desk. She looked in a small handheld vanity mirror while applying a peachy lip gloss with the other hand. She didn't have to glance up to feel my anxiety fill the room. "He, like, *just* parked, right? It takes at least ten minutes to walk from that visitor lot to our building."

"Yeah, but I'm a mess," I said quickly through swipes of deodorant and sprays of strawberry body mist. "I haven't seen him in a long time."

"Right, but he's just a friend, right?"

"A *best* friend," I snapped.

"Sure haven't talked about him much for a *best* friend," she said from the corner of her mouth. "Until recently, anyway."

"Sorry I don't share *every*thing from my past, Hannah. I'm trying to move forward." I rushed a silver liner against my tired eyes as I fumbled in my makeup bag for the blush.

"Geez. Chill, Cav. It's gonna be fine."

"If he doesn't have fun this weekend, or if he thinks I look bad or *whatever*, he's tight with my ex, and I just don't want that spreading around."

"Ohhhh, there's an ex in the picture?" She raised her eyebrows and looked up from the mirror. "Now, *this* is the most I've learned about your pre-Chicago self since I met you. Juicy. Evan should come here more often."

"Ethan," I stated loudly.

"Right, right. So, about this ex…"

"Nope. Not doing this now, Han. Sorry, I love you, but I'm not doing this. The past is in the past."

"Not when it drives three hours to see you," she offered through side-eye, holding back a grin. "This is gonna be a *fun* weekend!"

"Ugh, you're right. I never should've told him he could visit."

"I … never said that."

"What am I doing?" I wondered aloud. "No, it's fine," I said, very aware I was mostly just talking to myself at this point. "He agreed to leave Oakwood in Oakwood. That was our deal."

"Okay, but … have *you*?"

"Yes!" I yelled before she even finished her question. "Now, how do I look?"

"Hot. Skinny. Ready to party."

"Thanks," I said, continuing to fuss with my hair until a perky knock at the door pushed a lump into my throat. Hannah squealed and bounced toward the door. "Hannah! Wait!"

"Evan!" she sang as she swung the door open.

"Oh! Hello! Sorry, maybe I have the wrong room?" Ethan said, checking the number on the door again. "Does Andie Cavanaugh live here?"

"*Andie*?" Hannah buzzed. "Now, *that* is adorable."

Ethan blushed and scratched the back of his head while he studied Hannah.

"Cav, you didn't tell me he was so *cute*," she said, keeping her gaze on Ethan. I walked briskly toward them and nudged her out of the way.

"Hey," I offered quietly, my skin itching with an invigorating mix of fear and relief to see someone who looked every bit as Oakwood as I'd washed away these past few months.

"Andie?" he said, a smile starting to form across his face. I nodded, feeling the tears begin to glisten against my thick mascara.

Ethan tossed his duffle bag into the dorm room and scooped me up in a twirling bear hug.

"Oh my God," he said, setting me down as we both giggled. "You look…" His sky-blue eyes were wide as he absorbed the new me. "Different!" he finally said. "Your hair is … wow! So blonde! And you're *so* skinny, holy shit, Andrea."

"Thanks," I said.

"Not sure that was a compliment," Hannah whispered.

"No, it is?" Ethan guessed, still forming thoughts as he looked around the room. "Just … you deleted your Instagram, and I just didn't know you changed so much, but … good for you?" he guessed again. "I just, whatever, come here, you!" He grabbed me, rocking playfully side to side as his lean, lanky arms wrapped around my frail frame.

"This room is clutch," he said, nodding as he looked around.

"Thanks. How was your drive?" I asked.

"Oh, fine. Gave me a good excuse to catch up on some podcasts."

"Ahem," Hannah said loudly.

"Oh my gosh, sorry! Ethan, this is my roommate, Hannah."

"Nice to meet you," Ethan said, flopping onto my bed and kicking off his sneakers.

"Don't get too comfortable, Evan," Hannah said coyly. "Cav and I are gonna take you *out* tomorrow night."

"Cav?" he asked.

"Yeah, uh, that's me," I said sheepishly.

"Ohhh, like Cavanaugh, I get it," he said. "So if tomorrow's the big night out, what's the plan for tonight? We have, like … four months of catching up to do. And I have a *lot* of questions," he said through a soft laugh.

"Join the club," Hannah replied.

"Yeah, no, we'll catch up tomorrow," I offered. "I figured we just take it easy tonight, maybe watch a movie. Then tomorrow I'll show you around the city a bit, and later some of my friends from the restaurant are having a party. So tonight can be more chill."

"Perfect. I'm kinda tired from the drive."

I sat down softly next to Ethan on my bed.

"I missed you, Andie!" he said through an exaggerated side hug.

"I can't get over the 'Andie' thing. Just adorable." Hannah beamed.

"Yeah, yeah." I rolled my eyes and smiled. "I missed you, too, man," I said, leaning against Ethan's arm. He smelled like autumn. "Thanks for coming."

"Obviously!" He smiled. "You sure are dressed up for a chill night in."

"I am not." I blushed.

"She's been freaking out a little about you coming here," Hannah said.

"Hannah!" I shouted over Ethan and Hannah's laughter. "I have *not.*"

"No, it's cool. I'm just messing with you," Ethan said. "So, what're we watching tonight? *Pulp Fiction*?"

"Oh my God, you two are too much." Hannah snickered as she turned on the TV screen to show the opening of *Pulp Fiction* paused and ready to play.

"Nice!" Ethan and I burst into laughter. "Some things never change."

"Well, how could I not pick our favorite? At least

this time, we're not watching it in my parents' basement," I said, feeling the light form behind my eyes.

"Well, I'm going out. You two enjoy your weird movie." Hannah smiled. "I'll catch up with you tomorrow. You're not going to that Blush party without me."

"Yeah! Nice to meet you!" Ethan said.

The room felt small when Hannah left, and I was grateful to have the movie's sounds there to fill the air around us. I rested my head on Ethan's bony shoulder as my eyes got heavier.

"Hey, I'm falling asleep. Mind if I go to bed? You can keep watching if you want," I offered about halfway through the movie.

"Oh, sure, no worries. I'm beat, too. Where … do you want me to sleep?" he asked.

"You can sleep in my bed. Is that weird? I just mean, like, sleep *near* me, not *with* me. Sorry, is that weird?"

"After everything we've been through together, Andie, nothing's really 'weird' anymore." He turned off the TV and stretched out on my twin bed. "Just don't try any funny business, missy," he joked.

"Shut up," I said. "Let me just get ready." I grabbed my bathroom caddy, a baggy Death Cab for Cutie sweatshirt, and dark pajama pants. "Be right back."

In the bathroom, I washed all the heavy makeup off I'd just applied and swapped it for a lighter, more natural look. I pulled my hair into a messy bun, threw on the sweats, and ventured back to my dorm, where I climbed over Ethan to settle into the opposite end of the bed by the wall. He was lying on top of the covers, so I bundled underneath them.

"There she is," he said, staring at my more familiar face. He brushed his hand against my cheek, his blue eyes sparkling in the darkness. My body tensed, and I held my breath. "Love you, kid," he said softly before turning around. I exhaled and fell into a deep sleep, feeling safer than I had in years.

****

I got dressed and ready for the day before Ethan woke up.

"Good morning. Where did Andie go? She was *just* here in bed with me," he joked, waving toward my freshly applied bright makeup and fitted outfit.

"Shh!" I whispered, motioning to Hannah's bed, where she lay asleep. "And it's not morning. It's almost noon." I giggled quietly.

"Oh, snap!" Ethan shot out of bed. "We have a whole city to see!"

After he got ready, I showed Ethan all my favorite neighborhood spots, from the Thai bistro on Dearborn to the trendy record store on Madison. He followed me like a wide-eyed puppy, drinking in the city air as it hummed around us.

"You're so lucky that you live here," he said as we slurped yellow curry over lunch. "What about your job? What's it like there?"

"Oh, it's cool, I guess. They have a great open mic stage most nights. You'd love it."

"Yeah, I bet the local music scene here is huge."

"Yeah, I bet."

"Haven't you been to shows?" he asked.

"Mmm, not really," I replied. "It's just a lot with school and work."

"But what do you do for fun? The Andie I know would've already given me like ten demos of new local bands."

"I mean, I have fun!" I pressed. "I go out a lot with Hannah and some work people."

"Go out where?"

"Just wherever, usually someone's apartment."

"To do what?"

"Just hang out. I don't know, party?"

"Cool." Ethan nodded. "Well, what do you say tonight we ditch that Blush party and find a random local band we can check out? I am dying to see the scene here. I thought you'd be all over it already."

"No!" I stammered. "I-I want to take you to this party tonight. You wanted to see *my* Chicago, right? Plus, if we go to a club, we won't be able to drink or anything."

"So?"

"So, can you just trust me? It'll be fun. And this guy's place is really cool. I promise you'll love it. Okay?"

"Okay." Ethan shrugged. "As long as you swear we can still get Chicago deep dish for dinner tonight."

"I swear." I smiled. "So anyway, remember that *super* annoying girl from our old English class that would, like, shout the answers before Mr. Lazzarro could even finish the question?"

"Chloe Martin?"

"Yes! Chloe Martin! Well, I have a total Chloe Martin in my communications class. Her name is Rachel, and she is the *worst*. I think the professor hates her just as much as everyone else, but he has to be all diplomatic. It's a lot."

"Ha! I bet! Have you met anyone cool in your classes?"

"Hmm, not really. I mostly just hang out with Hannah and the people at work."

"Cool, cool," Ethan replied. "Hey, are you gonna finish your curry?"

"Oh, it was great, but I'm full."

"Looks like you barely touched it, but okay. More for me!" He switched our bowls and eagerly sipped the aromatic broth as he peppered me with more questions about city life.

Chapter Fifteen

By the time we got back to the dorm, we'd been roaming the South Loop for hours. Hannah was primping in the mirror to get ready for the Blush party that night when we walked in.

"My feet are sore! How do you guys walk this much all day?" Ethan laughed.

"Oh, Evan, don't let her fool you. She also lays around a *lot*," Hannah teased as I shot her a death glare.

"Pre-game time!" Hannah fluttered over with three shot glasses. I'd stopped asking what Hannah poured for me; it all tasted the same. We habitually clinked our drinks, and I quickly threw the fire down my throat in a single gulp, wincing at the burn and shaking it off. Hannah refilled ours and raised her eye to Ethan, frozen, his mouth hanging open for dramatic effect.

"Well, *that* was fast!" he said. I threw back the next shot, my lips pursing together as I let the sting warm my throat. "Jesus!" he exclaimed, his crystal-blue eyes melting from shock into worry.

"You joining us, hon?" Hannah giggled, the vodka quickly loosening her words and unknotting her hands as she ran them through her perfectly coiled hair.

"There is so much happening right now. I don't think I can process it." Ethan laughed. "I'm … good for now, I think. Seems like somebody should stay a *little* sober tonight if you guys are going hard?"

"Aww, don't ya wanna play?" Hannah teased, biting her lip. I shot her my don't-flirt-with-my-best-friend glance, but she deflected my judgmental gaze.

Ethan chuckled awkwardly and let out a loud exhale. "So, where are you two college girls taking me tonight?"

"It's not far," I said. "Just like a few blocks from here."

Ethan's phone buzzed, and he opened it quickly, sighing as he scrolled.

"Everything okay?" I asked.

"Sorry, yeah, just band stuff. The guys really want to open with this brand new song next weekend, and I just feel like we are *not* ready. And they won't shut up about it."

The warmth in my blood from the alcohol started to grow icy as the Oakwood poured from his mouth. I held my hand up and closed my eyes.

"Uh-uh, you promised, no Oakwood talk tonight," I reminded him.

Ethan looked up from his phone. "Right, but this isn't about *Oakwood*, Andie. This is about *me*. My life."

"I know, but, ugh, sorry, it's just weird hearing about the band. Can we talk about something else?"

Hannah scooted another shot toward me as she sensed the tension. I gratefully downed it, only wincing a little this time.

"Sure, yeah, okay." Ethan's voice dropped.

"Time to go!" Hannah exclaimed cheerily, trying to snap us back to the playful vibe from just moments earlier. I took the bait.

"Come on." I stood up, pulling Ethan off the bed with me. "College. Weekend. Chicago. What more does a small-town boy need?" I joked. "Let's go."

****

"Whose place is this again?" Hannah asked slowly, her words beginning to slur.

"Marco. He's a manager at Blush. His wife is a lawyer, and their place is *nice*," I offered.

"Yeah, it would seem so," Ethan said, his breath visible in the frozen air as we rang the buzzer outside a modern skyscraper. We heard the door click and hurried inside, stomping the frost from our shoes on the damp lobby rug. "Damn, maybe *I* need a lawyer wife," Ethan joked as we hopped into the velvet-padded elevator.

The walk from our dorm to the party had loosened the vibe as I gushed equally over lecture halls and cityscapes while Ethan listened attentively, soaking up each syllable. I felt his eyes dance when he looked at me, almost like he was looking in wide-eyed wonderment at a newly discovered species instead of chatting with an old friend, but I wore his admiration like a badge of honor.

"Well, so far, count me as impressed," Ethan stated as we got into the elevator. "I'm proud of you," he whispered. I felt myself start swaying softly.

"Thanks," I said, smiling. "I am, too."

Marco's apartment *was* huge and just as lavish as I'd heard it would be.

"You bougie bitch," Hannah laughed as we walked in.

"I can't help that my friends have good taste," I said through a silly British accent. Ethan elbowed me playfully.

"So when I picture the first year of college, I'm thinking like cheap beer in a shitty basement or something ... not this." He gestured to the sprawling digs with the giant windows overlooking a twinkling picturesque skyline.

"Trust me, ninety-nine percent of the time when Cav drags me to her work friends' places, it's *all* cheap beer and basements. *This* is not normal. But hell, I'll take it!"

I felt my face blush against Hannah's words.

"Ah! The truth comes out!" Ethan laughed.

"Well, whatever!" I said, my brain suddenly

unable to form an eloquent response.

"Cav! Jessica's here," Hannah whispered loudly in my ear.

"Nice! Go talk to her!" I said, pushing Hannah toward Jessica, the chatty new server at Blush, who was Hannah's latest crush.

"Shut up," she whispered. "Wish me luck." She flipped her hair behind one shoulder and pouted her lips as she parted the crowd to sashay toward her target.

"Oh. Hey, you." I heard Dean's familiar growl from behind me as he slipped his hand around my waist, his palm against my stomach. My body tensed as I felt his gristly beard prickle against my neck. "Was hoping you'd show." His skin reeked of whiskey.

Ethan instinctively grabbed Dean's arm, his eyes suddenly losing their sparkle amidst a now steely gaze.

"Whoa, who's this guy?" Ethan bellowed while Dean shook his arm out from under Ethan's grasp.

"What the fuck?" Dean grunted.

"Sorry! Are you okay?" I asked.

"Yeah," Dean and Ethan said in unison.

"She was talking to me," Ethan snapped.

"Uh, whatever, I'm too drunk for this." Dean stumbled backward.

"Ethan, this is Dean. We work together."

"You have a boyfriend you didn't tell me about?" Ethan said quietly.

"Ha!" Dean snorted from behind us. "No, no, just friends, dude. Who the hell are you anyway?"

"Seems pretty friendly..." Ethan said as he examined Dean's face.

"Dean, this is Ethan. He's my best friend from back home. He's visiting me this weekend."

"Whatever, just call me later if you wanna come over. If your guard dog will let you." He laughed through a breathy mumble before turning around and disappearing back into the crowd.

"Ow!" Ethan said as I smacked him on the arm.

"What are you *doing*?" I sneered. "That was so embarrassing!"

"Well, you could've given me a heads-up that you're sleeping with some bearded dude who's, like, forty. I thought he was just some stranger trying to creep on you."

"You don't have to protect me, Ethan." I rolled my eyes. "I've been taking care of myself just fine these past few months."

"I get it, Andie, but you can't blame me for being a little taken aback when some random old guy starts grinding on you. As your friend, it's kinda my job to look out for you."

"Oh, really? Why start now?" The words fell out of my mouth before I could stop them. I closed my eyes in instant remorse.

"What is *that* supposed to mean?" Ethan said directly, pausing slightly between each word.

"Nothing, I'm sorry. I've been drinking. I didn't mean anything by that. Can we just forget it? And forget Dean. He's nobody. That's why I didn't tell you about him."

Ethan was looking down and shaking his head. "Seems like we should go somewhere and talk."

"No! There's nothing to talk about. Can we just have fun? Look, I'm sorry I said that. It just came out. Come on, you know I love you."

Ethan looked around the room as he pondered what to say next, his jaw tensing as he thought. Before he could speak, Hannah came bursting back toward us with three red plastic cups sloshing with some kind of fruity mixed drink.

"You guys should come to the dining room. It's getting crazy in there!" she shouted, handing us each a cup. Ethan set his softly on a nearby side table while I closed my eyes and swallowed as much of it as I could before the sour flavor overwhelmed me.

"Hell yeah, Cav! Come on, there's a dance party going on in that room. Let's goooo," she sang, grabbing my hand as she started walking away, trying to drag me along as Jessica waved her back, drawing Hannah toward the hype. My eyes shot toward Ethan, who had finally met my gaze again, tilting his head as if trying to figure me out but not being able to quite get there. I dropped Hannah's hand.

"I'm just gonna get some air with Ethan real quick," I said.

"What? Boo! We *just* got here!" Hannah exclaimed as she started playfully dancing to the heavy beat that was pounding from the next room. Glitter and lavender body mist shook from her bouncy curls as she rocked her head to the music.

"Yeah, yeah, you stay. We'll be right back," I said, hoping that it was true.

"Don't be long!" she yelled as she slipped into the crowded, dimly lit dining room. I wandered back toward Ethan and motioned my head toward the door. As we stepped into the hall, the air felt suddenly thick and quiet. We didn't say much in the elevator and eventually found a bench on the sidewalk out front. Ethan dusted the frost from the seat, and I gingerly sat down. *It's just Ethan*, I reminded myself. *Nothing to be scared of. I'll just tell him I didn't mean it. He can't stay mad at me.*

"Look," Ethan started, his chilly blue eyes piercing my skin. I cringed in anticipation. "I'm not mad at you. Honestly, I'm kinda mad at *me*."

"Huh?" I asked through a puzzled stare.

"You weren't wrong with what you said. I didn't protect you before, ya know, with Josh."

"I don't want to talk about him," I said quickly. "You promised we wouldn't…"

"Andie, please. Just let me talk."

I paused, biting my lip and feeling my eyes start to glisten.

"I was *friends* with Josh. I had no idea he was such a monster. But, ugh, I mean, I saw him treat you like shit. Everybody kinda did. And I should've stood up for you more than I did. Ever since you moved away, I can't stop thinking that I let you down."

"You didn't. It's fine," I lied, desperately hoping to crawl out of the conversation. "We're good, I promise."

"Well, cool. Thanks. But I just need you to know I'm sorry. I guess I just didn't let myself realize how bad it had gotten for you. I mean, if he was that bad in public, I can't imagine what it must've been like in private."

"It's fine," I said again before he could finish that thought. "Look at me! I'm good! I don't even think about him," I lied again.

"That's good," Ethan replied. "I mean, I know you've already had another relationship since then. Things seemed good with you and Carter for a long time, so at least Josh isn't, like, your last memory of a boyfriend. I know it ended shitty with Carter, and I'm sure it sucks knowing he's with Olivia now, but at least you have some good memories with him, right? That would be easier to move on from than that piece of shit, Josh."

My ribs ached, and my fingernails dug into my palm until I felt the skin break. "Carter is with Olivia now?" I tried to level my shaky voice.

"Well, yeah … for a while now. You didn't

know?"

I shook my head, afraid of what might come out if I opened my mouth.

"Oh, sorry, I guess you've really been disconnected, huh?"

I nodded softly through racing thoughts that came in and out so quickly I couldn't pin anything down. I felt small drops of blood pool from my palm where my fingernails had dug, so I wiped them against the softly fallen snow that glistened against my dark wool coat.

"I'm sorry, Andie, I thought you knew. But who cares about Carter, right? Look at you here, big city, cool job. You won. Forget him. That wasn't what I wanted to talk about. I just wanted to apologize for everything I didn't do when Jo—"

I couldn't hear that name again. I couldn't think about Olivia Schroeder's tanned bikini body gliding against Carter. I couldn't think about how being with her had probably erased me from every part of his mind. When you stare at perfection every day, it's pretty easy to forget about the broken. It had ended with Carter precisely as I'd predicted from the beginning—a pretty, fit, exotic goddess reminded him what he deserved, and he was likely sick of trying to fix me. I didn't blame him, but it didn't stop the pain from absorbing my breath.

I needed Ethan to stop talking before "Josh" or "Carter" escaped his mouth again, so I plunged my lips onto his, surprising us both with my spontaneity. It worked. He had stopped talking. And we weren't thinking about Josh or Carter anymore.

At first, Ethan's smooth, narrow lips tensed against my kiss and then softened but froze.

"Just shut up and kiss me back," I whispered, kissing him again. His breath shallowed, and he brought his hand to my face, cradling my jaw in his gentle hold as he finally returned my enthusiasm with his sincere, eager lips.

I had always been a little curious what it would feel like to kiss Ethan, but had shrugged it off as thinking it would probably feel like kissing my brother. It didn't.

Ethan pulled back, his eyes brimming wild with questions. "Are you... What are you... I mean..." he stuttered. I pulled his face back toward me and kissed him again. This time I welcomed the quiet that surrounded us. It was safe and steady. I started to drift out of my skin, as though I was watching from the sky as two teenagers made out on a park bench while snowflakes flurried against the city lights. It looked like a movie.

I didn't know what would happen next. I hadn't thought that far ahead. But for a fleeting moment, the past was over, and the future wasn't real yet. I was deeply grounded in the present as Ethan's arresting, nostalgic touch pulsated through my body.

He pulled back softly again to take a breath, his forehead resting on mine. His sweet, focused eyes were centered on me as my body shook from the cold, exhilaration, and impending guilt.

"Andie, I don't know what to say," he started.

"Please stop calling me that," I said, running my lips over his sharp, smooth jawline.

"What? Why? I always call you Andie." He smiled as I slid my fingers through his messy hair.

"That's not me anymore," I replied.

"But ... I love that part of you. It's always been us, Ethan and Andie."

"That part of me is dead," I said bluntly, the words once again spilling from my mouth before any form of social restraint could be engaged.

Ethan grabbed my shoulders and pulled me back.

"Whoa, don't say that," he said, brushing his fingers against my cold, sunken cheek.

I'd opened the gates again, giving the invitation to talk about the dark, twisty things I couldn't talk about yet. I had to act fast to pull us back out from this dangerous place we were inching toward.

I leaned in and whispered gently in his ear.

"Let's go back to my place and turn this up a notch." I tried to keep my voice breathy and soft.

Ethan scooted back from me, toward the edge of the bench. He placed his elbows on his knees and hung his head.

"This is not what you want," he said, unable to look at me.

"Of course it is." My hand slid over his thigh. He pushed it away.

"Stop, Andrea. Come on. Haven't you ever thought about us like this? I know I have. But I never wanted to mess up our friendship. Because it's always been you, Andie. And in some ways it always will be. You're my best friend, and as … surreal and fun as it feels to kiss you, it's like, I can't lose you. And I don't think you really want this for us, either. This is some voodoo shit you're trying to do to me here, and while kissing you and feeling you like this is something I've definitely wanted, this is not *how* I ever wanted it."

The frozen air suddenly felt sweltering, and the night sky was quickly closing in. My hands started to shake as I tightened my face to keep the tears from forming. I had no words.

"You … are not you," he continued. "And the worst part is, I think that's on purpose. I came here to be with my friend Andie, not whoever this is."

"It's still me," I whispered, wiping a stubborn tear from my cheek.

"It's not. And you don't want it to be. Which sucks, Andie, because you're pretty great. And, like, everyone else knows that but you."

His words hung in the air and hit me harder with each breath. I didn't have the energy to bury this with the rest of my wreckage. It was too heavy now. So I let them pierce through me, bending toward the pain.

"I think I'm just gonna drive home tonight," Ethan said.

"No, stay until tomorrow. That was our plan," I pleaded.

He shook his head as he stood up. "No, I need some space, okay? You'll walk home with Hannah, right? Promise you won't walk alone?"

I nodded sheepishly, feeling like a stupid kid playing dress-up underneath this suffocating outfit and dense makeup.

"All right. I'll see you later, Andrea," Ethan said as he typed the parking lot address into the maps app on his phone, walking in long strides away from the cold bench where I sat. My full name sounded formal and unfamiliar in his voice. I watched him walk until he disappeared into the frosty night. He was gone, and I suddenly ached for him and his lanky side hugs, joyous laughter, and pensive conversations over bad diner lattes.

What have I done? I thought. *I just burned down my safe place.* Any last shred of who I once was had disappeared with Ethan in the frozen, dark air. And all that was left was this brightly dyed shell I didn't recognize.

I then remembered Carter and Olivia and felt queasy, my stomach churning as I pictured them together and happy. There was too much I didn't want to think about. It was getting hard to keep track of what needed to be pushed down, and I was running out of space.

The front door of the apartment building swung open in front of me, and I heard Dean's familiar, low laughter pile out as he stumbled onto the sidewalk, a dark-haired woman in a short dress following closely behind him. He wrapped his coat around her shoulders and slung his arm around her waist as she giggled and chattered while they weaved down the road to look for a cab. I let out a breath of relief when it was clear he hadn't seen me. I think I hated Dean—not because of the other woman, just ... because.

What have I done? I repeated in my head, the question swelling as I watched Dean and his new acquaintance practically fall into a nearby yellow taxi, laughing at their own stupor.

I couldn't go back to the party. But I couldn't stay on this bench, either. My skin was itching to move, and my mind was itching to forget. So I started walking briskly in the direction of my dorm, bundling under my coat and unsure if the chill or the angst was the cause of my incessant shivering.

Hannah was still at the party, so I texted her that I was leaving. My conscience nagged at me to stay and make sure she was okay, but the selfish desperation won, as it so often did lately. I ignored the seeping guilt and hurried to my room, letting my coat fall to the floor and leaving my clothes, shoes, and makeup on as I climbed atop the comforter and closed my eyes tight, praying for sleep and forgiveness to wash over me.

Chapter Sixteen

My eyes slowly flickered open the next morning as the sun peered cruelly through the purple cotton curtains.

"Hannah!" I shouted through a dry voice and thumping headache. The familiar grumble that came from her bed was enough to let me know she was home. I let out a tense breath of gratitude. Feeling her presence nearby somehow lessened the gnawing guilt that came from my tactless retreat in the night. Maybe she wouldn't remember that I left her.

There was a tall glass of water in a green plastic cup and two Advil tablets on my bedside table. I hoped that meant she wasn't too mad. I guzzled the water in quick gulps as it cooled my parched, raw throat, and then slumped back against my pillow.

What have I done? I asked myself again, this time with a horrifically clearer mind. I closed my eyes and saw last night all over again, watching myself ruin a sacred friendship on a cold park bench. I wondered if Ethan drove all the way home in the middle of the night or if he'd stopped somewhere to sleep. I wondered if he'd made it home and if he'd started telling people what a mess of smeared mascara, scrawny shoulders, and thoughtless lips I was. The humiliation was palpable in my chest, spreading through my veins like poison.

I wanted to text Ethan and try to explain, but I had nothing left to say, and I wasn't even sure which side of me would be saying it. My champagne highlights felt suddenly like cheap box dye, and the fresh bronzer stains on my pillow disgusted me.

What the hell am I doing? I asked myself. I started pulling off the clothes I'd worn last night that began to look like a costume I'd never seen before. My skin began to sweat under the tight fabric, and I became desperate to undress, tearing at the material and kicking it deep under my bed until I could finally breathe again.

I quietly raided my dresser until I found an oversized Jack's Mannequin t-shirt underneath the knockoff designer brands I'd bought with my Blush money. I slipped the t-shirt on and closed my eyes as I remembered excitedly buying it at their concert in Detroit last year with Ethan. That had been an epic night I hadn't thought about in months. We'd elbowed our way to the front row and watched Andrew McMahon, our music idol, pour his heart out as he pounded on the piano. We were so close we could see the sweat beads fall from his forehead onto the keys, and we screamed every word at the top of our lungs, forgetting about the world.

I breathed in the t-shirt as if it still somehow smelled like that stuffy, crowded concert hall. I opened my eyes again to see a stranger in this hallowed shirt staring at me from the dresser mirror. I turned, unable to look at the blonde monster who had pushed my best friend away, leaving him alone in the cold, starry night. I pulled on some sweat shorts and climbed back into bed.

I grabbed my phone to see if Ethan had texted me, but then quickly dropped it when I saw the words *1 NEW E-MAIL FROM: JOSH MACMILLAN* peer back at me. I couldn't breathe. My phone now looked like a poisonous snake hissing at me from the comforter and, though I couldn't touch it, I was too petrified to move, either. My mind sprinted in every direction, but no single thought had time to stick. I gasped for air as I returned to my body, suddenly needing urgently to know what it said.

I swiped open my phone with shaky hands, and

there it was.

> *To: Andrea Cavanaugh*
> *From: Josh MacMillan*
> *Subject: hi.*
>
> *hey andie ... i know it's been a while but i had a dream about you last night. i was resting my head on your lap while you stroked my hair. it was beautiful. how are you?*

I tried to stand up, but my knees buckled from underneath me. I steadied myself against the wall, sliding down until I was sitting on the floor by my bed. My phone dropped from my hands, thumping against the hardwood. I began scratching at my forearm incessantly, clawing at my skin to let the poison out but just leaving red, ragged streaks instead.

"He's everywhere," I heard myself say. "He's never going away." My voice started to get louder as my chest burned, threatening to bubble up everything I'd been pushing down. It had never gone away; it just lay semi-dormant, churning in its own toxicity, mixing with the other thoughts and growing bigger under the pressure while it plotted a dramatic escape from my body. "He's everywhere!" I choked, tasting the acid at the back of my throat.

"Cav?" Hannah's worried voice shot through the dense air, but she sounded miles away through the ringing in my ears.

"Don't touch me!" I screamed as Hannah's gentle hand on my knee felt like nails against a chalkboard.

"Whoa, okay, you're okay. I'm here. I won't touch you. What's wrong?" Hannah was kneeling by me now, her brown eyes deep with panic, her dark curls nestled under a purple silk scarf. "You're scaring me, Cav. What's going on? Do you need me to call someone?"

"No!" I yelled through the tears that stung my haunted eyes. "It's him. I thought he was gone. I thought I got away, but I didn't, Hannah. And I never will."

"Okay, deep breaths. *Who* is here?" Her head turned to scan the room, and she looked back at me with a quick head shake. "Nobody is here, hon. You're okay. Who is where?"

"Not here, *here*." I pounded my chest with a closed fist, falling defeated onto Hannah's lap as I sobbed. Her body released the tension, and she cradled my hollow frame in her strong, lean arms, slowly rocking back and forth.

"Hon, I don't know what you're saying. Take a deep breath and talk to me. You're not alone," she said calmly.

I tried to inhale, but the breath came in sharp, quick stutters instead of the long, slow sweeps I craved. The dam was breaking.

"Josh. It's Josh." His name tasted bitter and wicked against my tongue. "He e-mailed me. He… He's an ex. And he … he was … awful," I managed to say.

"Okay, no problem, I'm here. He sounds like a jerk, huh?"

I nodded slowly. "He would… He hurt me. A lot."

"Oh, hell no," Hannah replied. "Okay, so he's a *real* asshole."

"And, and nothing was supposed to happen, but after we broke up he … he … and I didn't stop him. And it hurt. It hurt so bad. And then he left, and I haven't seen him. But he just e-mailed me. He's *thinking* about me. I can't get him off of me. It's been over a year, and I can't get him off of me." I started scratching at my arm again, more vigorously this time as if I could scrub him out from under my skin.

"Whoa, whoa, stop, stop, look at me," Hannah coaxed. I looked at her, my shell melting and exposing the darkness that seeped from the cracks through each word. "This is not your fault," she said slowly and directly. I hung my head again, my aching body unable to meet her gaze. "No, you look at me." She pulled my chin up. "This. Is. Not. Your. Fault. And he can e-mail you all he wants, but he is *not* here, and he has *no* power over you, okay?"

"How do you know?" I sputtered meekly.

"Because if it were true that our rapists have power over us forever, then I'd be doomed."

I winced at the R-word. I was still unable to say it out loud. I had said no, but I hadn't fought him. I hadn't thrown him off of me. I'd lain there, paralyzed by fear. Having been beaten down by his words and hands for so long, I had just accepted my fate in that moment on the blue couch. So the idea of being a victim of an abusive guy didn't resonate with me. If I had been more assertive, less eager to please, more worthy of being loved gently and sweetly, *anything*, then *everything* could've been different.

Hannah paused, took a sharp inhale, and continued. "And I refuse to be doomed by some piece of shit that thought it was okay to have sex with an unconscious drunk girl."

My eyes widened. "You?" I asked. She nodded.

"Last year," she offered.

"What did... What did you do?" I asked, wiping my face with my arm, suddenly having the energy to sit up taller.

Hannah shrugged. "Nothing, really. I mean, stopped hanging out with *that* guy for one." She laughed awkwardly. "But I just ... tried to move on, I guess."

"Did you tell anyone?" I asked.

She shook her head. "It's nobody's business."

I nodded.

"And I'm okay," she said. "I barely think about him, and I certainly don't let that one night run my life. You just have to move on and push through it. I find it's best to just stay busy."

"I can't keep pushing. I can't push anymore. Trust me, I'm not okay. And I don't know what to do." I slumped back against the wall, too tired to keep crying.

"Come on, yes, you do. Delete that e-mail, stand up, get dressed, and just move on, one thing at a time. Sometimes that's what it takes, getting through one thing at a time until days and weeks go by and you realize you haven't even thought about it."

I shook my head weakly. "It's not that easy."

"It is," Hannah said, her voice breaking. "It is because ... because it *has* to be."

"It's not," I whispered. "This isn't just something that happened to me. It's like it's become *part* of me. And I can't get it out."

Hannah forcefully wiped a teardrop from her cheekbone and stood up.

"I gotta take a shower. Sorry, it's already, like, noon. Just ... take some deep breaths, and we'll go out tonight and have some fun, okay? Get your mind off of things. It'll be good for you."

I nodded silently, unable to look at Hannah as she hurriedly grabbed her towel and scented body wash, tripping over some piles of loose clothes on the floor on her way to the door.

"The best way to get over one guy is to get under another." She forced a laugh as she opened the door to the hallway. "I promise we'll have fun tonight, okay?"

I heard the door close behind her, and I tensed at the loud click as she scurried to lock it. I looked at my phone on the floor in front of me, staring at the blank screen as it begged me to swipe it open and see the message that threatened to loom over me in a poisonous fog for as long as I was alive. I picked it up slowly, closed my eyes, and swiped it open, tapping the home button over and over to ensure that by the time my eyes opened, the e-mail would be gone. It was, and I let out a breath of stale, toxic air. I typed out the text before I could find a million reasons to stop myself.

Me: **I'm not okay. I need help.**

I waited for the worst to happen. I expected denial or panic or questions I wasn't ready to answer, but instead, her response sent warmth back into my veins in a mix of aggravated relief and instinctive hesitation.

Mom: **I just transferred money into your account for a train ticket. The next train leaves in two hours. Come home. It will be okay.**

I didn't pack a bag. I didn't leave a note for Hannah. I grabbed the fancy sequined clutch I'd used the night before that still held my wallet and keys, threw my phone in there, pulled on my snow boots, and left. I didn't feel the frozen air against my exposed skin as my feet crunched against the frosted sidewalk. I didn't acknowledge the familiar stabs of hunger that heaved within my stomach. I just staggered toward Union Station until I found myself barreling toward Oakwood like a moth drawn to the flickering light of an electric fence. If facing this meant I had to get hurt again and again to make it stop, I would. I couldn't keep fighting to ignore it.

Chapter Seventeen

My mom tried not to appear startled when she saw me, but she'd always had a terrible poker face. Her fingers dug into my back as she hugged me sharply. I hadn't said much by the time we got into her car, heading back to my parents' house from the Oakwood train station.

"It's going to be okay, Andrea," my mom said as she drove, weaving her gaze back and forth from the road to my face, her knuckles white as they gripped the steering wheel.

I rested my head against the cold window of the passenger seat, my shallow breath fogging the glass as the intrusively familiar landscapes flew by.

"But what if it's not?" I asked quietly, studying my finger as it traced against the frosty windowpane. My mom didn't reply, but I felt her searching for the right words. I turned to look at her, settling back deeper into my seat. "What if it's not?" I asked again, needing an answer. "Is that okay, too?"

"Andrea, honey, we will do whatever we need to do. When we get home, why don't you write down the name and number of the therapist you've been seeing at school, okay? I'll have Dr. Hawthorne give them a call, and we'll get everything figured out."

"I haven't been going," I said bluntly, the honesty waving over me like a soft, warm blanket. "Actually, I haven't been to therapy since I got to Chicago." I became more brazen with each word. "I don't want to keep talking about the past, Mom. But I just … can't … *feel* this way anymore."

I think we both anticipated tears, but none came. I couldn't look at my mother's hurt expression, so I closed my eyes instead.

"I'm sorry. I don't really feel well, and I didn't sleep much last night. Can I just lay down for a bit when we get home?"

"Yes," my mom replied softly. "And please let your professors know you won't be in class tomorrow."

"I already e-mailed them on the train saying I'd be out all week," I vaguely remembered out loud.

"Oh, okay. Great," my mom said.

I felt myself start to doze off against the window and drifted upstairs to my old bedroom once we got home. The walls were half bare with outlines of ripped tape stuck where my mom had quietly removed every shred of physical evidence that Carter Wells had existed. I was too exhausted to be sad.

I fell onto my bed and breathed in the aroma of my Oakwood bedroom, feeling the nervous, giggling energy of junior high sleepovers with Stephanie or getting lost in my favorite songs with Ethan while we picked apart the lyrics and played video games.

Before I could smile at the nostalgia, I was hit with a flashback of Josh as he yanked my head back by my hair because I'd nervously pulled at his t-shirt while we made out, causing the neckline to stretch. When I did it again unconsciously, he threw me off the bed. We had to kiss with my arms tucked behind my pillow after that, which he loved. I pushed the pillow off my bed in disgust, my stomach frothing at the cruel reminder.

I laid my head down flat on the bed, praying that the lingering memory of his dry, chapped lips against my skin would dissipate. My aching body eventually gave in to the sleep and was comfortably swallowed by slumber for a few hours.

"Andie…" a sweet voice loudly whispered. I didn't have to open my eyes to know it was Stephanie.

She smelled like apple blossoms, and her voice rang distinctly like an old favorite song. I slowly came back to my body as I awoke, inch by inch, sitting up when I saw Steph sitting at the end of my bed.

"Hey, you..." she said, her green eyes light and misty. "Your mom called me. I came over right after class. I'm sorry to wake you up."

"Is she up?" my mom asked from the hallway, poking her head into my room.

"Yeah, come on in," Stephanie offered. I nodded, pulling my legs to my chest. My mom walked softly and slowly before eventually sitting nearby at my desk chair.

"You didn't have to come. I'm sorry—" I started before Stephanie shushed me.

"Hey, stop, I wanted to come. It's been a long time."

I nodded sheepishly. I couldn't even remember the last time I had texted her.

"So, hey, I may not know what's been going on in Chicago, and you definitely look ... well ... different, but there is one person I know for sure who can catch me up, and that's Andie Cavanaugh from Oakwood, Michigan. *You* may not remember her, though? Does that name ring a bell? Ya know, that tall, cute chick with crazy red highlights? Loves music and animals and weird movies?"

I smiled as I felt a light form behind my eyes.

"Ohhh, see, Mrs. C? She's still in there." Stephanie laughed as my mom tried poorly to pretend she wasn't holding back tears.

"Anyway, we thought you might need a reminder because the Andie *we* know is pretty great. See for yourself." Stephanie pulled a small box from the floor and set it gently on the bed in front of me, motioning for me to go through it.

I felt my lips curve into a wide grin as I began to rummage through the items they'd collected. On top of the small heap was the gold medal my high school jazz band had won at the state festival. My fingers traced the outline of the engraved words and starchy blue ribbon that it hung from. If I closed my eyes, I could picture myself there, a ball of nervous energy draped in a heavy black gown, praying I wouldn't miss the cue for my vibraphone solo. I didn't. We all wore our medals to school the next day. The kids who drove luxury cars and played soccer would roll their eyes at us down the hallway, but the solidarity of our band's unified pride was too rich even for their blood. It was a mood, and we felt like kings for a day. I took a deep breath as if I could taste the victory one more time.

Next, I came across a clipping from an op-ed article I'd written for the school newspaper about anti-feminism in modern romantic comedies. There had been some heated reactions when it first came out. I could still feel the thrill in my spine when I pictured the debates it started in the cafeteria. That article was the beginning of my passion to study journalism. As my eyes quickly gazed through the printed paragraphs, I could barely remember having once written such beautiful musings.

"Man, I was pretty good, huh?" I said through a soft laugh.

"*Are* good. You *are* pretty good, Andie," Stephanie corrected me.

Next in the box was a stuffed dog from my childhood, with mismatched button eyes my grandma had sewn on after our real dog had chewed them off. I brought the stuffed dog to my face to feel its plush fur against my cheek and inhaled deeply as if my grandmother's vanilla-cedar perfume was still somehow enmeshed behind the buttons.

Next, an autographed poster from the Dashboard Confessional concert I went to for my sixteenth birthday. Ethan and I had waited outside the venue for two hours until the front man came out and signed it. I was freezing in my pleated leopard skirt, but I didn't care. We sang Dashboard songs loudly with the other diehard fans who knew that a glimpse of Chris Carrabba was worth the subzero wait. My fingers traced over his signature, and I could feel Ethan's exuberance fill my heart as I thought of us skipping over ice patches back to our car with our freshly signed poster as if it were a winning lottery ticket.

Lastly in the box was half of a heart-shaped friendship bracelet that Stephanie had saved since we were kids. The silver was tarnished, and the paint was chipped, but it still hung proudly from its weathered chain. I felt my eyes sting with tears as I remembered buying these together in middle school and swearing we'd keep them forever. I lost mine a couple years later, but Stephanie never did.

The box was empty now, and Stephanie took a deep breath.

"Now I want to make sure you noticed that this is an Andie box," she started. "Not a Josh's ex-girlfriend box, not a Carter's ex-girlfriend box. This is an Andie box. This is *you*, girl. Remember your crazy-ass pink hair?" She laughed, scrolling through the photos in her phone until she found one from sophomore year where I was beaming goofily into the camera with my freshly dyed cotton-candy-hued hair. "You didn't care that we all thought you were nuts. You *loved* it. And you *rocked* it." She picked up the newspaper clipping. "And this article you wrote was ballsy as hell. You are a *force*, Andie. And those guys were just blips on your magnificent radar, okay?"

I stared through Stephanie as my mind flooded

with memories. Before I could speak, she leaned in and hugged me tightly.

"I don't care if you don't want me to hug you right now. This is happening." We both laughed. "Please don't forget that pink-haired weirdo. No man can erase her. Only you can do that," she whispered. I let my body unclench in her petite, snug hold, and she motioned for my mom to come over, who happily wrapped us both in her warm, soft arms.

"Thank you," I said earnestly as we separated. "For reminding me that I'm more than just somebody's girlfriend. Or ex-girlfriend. And for reminding me that I used to have *really* cool hair." I laughed as Stephanie threw a pillow at me.

"Don't get any ideas," my mom teased. "I thought your father was going to have a heart attack when you came out of the bathroom with that pink hair." She chuckled, wiping her streaky mascara from under her eyes as she cleaned the lenses of her smudged glasses against her sweater. "Thank you for being here, Stephanie," my mom said as she rested her hand on Stephanie's slender shoulder. "You're a good friend."

"I'll be honest. It hasn't been super easy to be your friend lately, Andie, but at the end of the day, I just want you to be okay."

"I know, I know. Thanks, Steph," I said awkwardly, suddenly feeling the weight of the attention in the room. "Hey, did you ... did you happen to tell Ethan I'm here?" I asked.

"Oh, yeah, I actually called him on my way over to see if he wanted to meet me here, but he ... declined. Sorry."

"No, no, it's okay. I guess I shouldn't be surprised. I think I really messed up." I hung my head as last night flashed before me. "And I don't know how to fix it."

"Dr. Hawthorne has agreed to see you tomorrow afternoon," my mom offered. "Your dad and I would really like you to go. I think she helped you a lot last year. You don't have to promise me any certain outcome. Just promise me you'll go. Even if you just sit there for an hour, just promise me you'll go."

Stephanie nodded along as my mom talked. I felt the urge in my chest to drone through a long list of reasons why that wasn't necessary, but the lie tasted acrid on my tongue as I tried to spit it out, so instead, I just surrendered, nodding heavily and promising to try.

Chapter Eighteen

I nervously tapped my fingers in comforting rhythms against the pleather couch in Dr. Hawthorne's waiting room the next day. I couldn't find a comfortable position, so instead just manically flipped through old Oprah magazines that were sprawled on the glass coffee table in front of me. The pages were worn, and the bindings were stretched, but I was grateful to have something to keep my hands busy as the minutes ticked by.

As I pretended to be deeply immersed in an article about low-calorie holiday appetizers, I jumped in my seat when a familiar voice called my name gently. I scurried into Dr. Hawthorne's office without making eye contact with the other people in the waiting room. I'd hoped they thought I was just there as a visitor, waiting for my broken friend to come out of one of the offices, but the secret was out. These faceless, damaged strangers now knew that I was one of them, too.

"It's great to see you, Andrea," Dr. Hawthorne said as she settled down into her creaky wooden desk chair. Her black-rimmed round glasses kept scooting down her nose as she focused on me, scribbling some early notes on her yellow legal pad without even looking down. Her navy-blue tunic was adorned with a muted pastel scarf that seemed to match the colors of the throw pillows on her couch that I flopped down on, pulling my knees to my chest to take up as little space as possible.

"Thanks. You, too," I said, my gaze darting around the room as I bit my lip and tapped my fingers into those familiar, soothing patterns. As I saw her start writing again, I quickly tucked my hands under the cuffs of my long sleeves, squeezing and releasing the fabric into the same patterns, hoping she'd hold back on any comments about my restless hands.

"How have things been? How are you?" she asked.

"Well, I think my mom probably caught you up to speed," I said, glancing at the clock. Dr. Hawthorne shook her head.

"No, not really. I think part of the concern is that your mom doesn't even really know how you're doing, so there wasn't much for her to tell me."

"Ah, good point," I said through a forced laugh. "Umm, to be honest…"

"*To be honest* is typically something people say right before they lie. Let's do each other both a favor and claim this hour as the safe, confidential place that it is. I will respect you by listening and doing whatever it is I can to help. But, to do that, you have to respect me enough to be honest." She paused and smiled warmly. "What do you think?"

My mind started searching for the lies I usually had ready to launch, from "I'm doing great" to "I've totally moved on" and countless others, but as I opened my mouth to let one fall out, instead, there was only silence. My body was rejecting the dishonesty and stifling the words before they could reach the air. I tried again, but nothing came out.

"I'm…" I began, my eyes widening as if surprised by the sound of my own voice. "Scared," I said, breathing some of the tension out of my body and into the drafty office.

"Okay. What do you feel scared of?"

I stared at Dr. Hawthorne through squinted eyes as I worried about what might come out next. I felt my ribs part as they prepared for something, anything, to pour out of me.

"I'm… We have, like, doctor-patient confidentiality or something, right? Like you can't tell my parents what I tell you? Or anyone? Right?" I needed confirmation before I let the darkness spill onto another person.

"That's right. Unless you say you're thinking about harming yourself or somebody else, then I am bound by the law to keep our conversation private."

"Okay," I said, feeling the vault crack and the skeletons unearth from the shallow graves I'd dug in haste and horror. "But I don't know where to start. It's a lot. And I think you're going to be mad at me because I haven't been going to therapy. I just wanted to be okay." My voice began to break.

"Andrea," she said gently. "The way I see it is, you have two choices right now. One is that you can keep everything inside your body that you've been thinking and feeling that is causing you pain, and just let it stay there and see when and how it inevitably comes out. Or you can get it out of your body now by saying it out loud. Your mind can be like … like a bad neighborhood at night. Don't walk through it alone." She laughed lightly. "It's better to give some of this back to the universe and to someone you trust who is trained to accept it from you. And I promise I am up to the challenge. But if you keep these intrusive thoughts to yourself, they will only continue to haunt you."

In what felt like one long breath, I exhaled everything I could think of into the room as Dr. Hawthorne listened intently, nodding and scribbling notes as she kept her eyes focused on me, leaning in for some parts and stretching back and crossing her legs for others.

I can't remember exactly what I said as I felt myself floating above my body for most of it, but I know

I told her about Dean and how I hated him but hated myself more for needing him. I told her that Josh was in my head daily, hourly, continuing to berate me and scar me from worlds away and how every time I saw a man with unkempt hair and brown corduroys or heard someone raise their voice, I'd freeze like a hunted animal, waiting for him to appear and finish me. I told her about Hannah and how weird it felt to be close to someone that knew nothing about me. We talked about my exhaustion, compulsions, poor nutrition, and binge drinking. And I was lighter with every word.

She didn't scream in horror when I told her I drank too much. She didn't run out of the room when I described the constant shame that hung over me like a heavy cloak. Nothing I said appeared to surprise her or even cause an eyebrow raise, which only empowered me to go deeper and deeper until the comfort of land was just a distant speck against a long, choppy horizon.

"Thank you for being honest, Andrea. And thank you for trusting me," she said after I finally paused long enough to catch my breath.

"You don't think I'm crazy? Or weird? Or some kind of a monster?" I asked.

"No," she said bluntly. "I think that what you are describing is completely understandable behavior and thought patterns for an eighteen-year-old who has been through the traumatic events that you experienced in your abusive relationship with Josh."

I winced at the sound of his name. She noticed.

"But it's not just that," I said. "Something started that. Something wrong with *me* is what put me in that situation in the first place. Look, I know he is a bad guy. I get that now. I know what he did was wrong, but … I also know that I let him. That I … must have somehow believed I deserved it or something. Or that I was really just so unlovable that it made it easier for him. I don't know. But I know that you always call *him* the abuser and *me* the survivor, but it doesn't always feel that way. I feel like if I hadn't been so ... I don't know ... *me*, that this wouldn't have happened the way it did."

"Andrea, it's likely that Josh has his own traumatic past. I have no way of knowing that for sure, of course, but usually abusers come from some kind of abusive or otherwise difficult childhood where they learn these patterns. Have you ever heard the expression 'only hurt people hurt people?' Anyway, my point is that wherever he may have learned it from, that it was okay to treat a partner like that, he groomed you into it. It was slow, methodical, and purposeful. He was charming. He gained your trust, and he planted seeds until you felt like, instead of questioning his motives, it was *you* who was losing your mind. It's really not dissimilar to how cult leaders work. But look, if you go back to school, I am going to strongly recommend you attend a support group for survivors of sexual assault and domestic abuse."

"A support group?" I asked through clenched teeth.

"Yes. How close do you live to the YWCA on LaSalle in Chicago?"

I shrugged.

"Well, I'll get you the address. They have a really fantastic program. I have a former colleague who practices there now and speaks highly of it."

"What would that be like?"

"Freeing," she responded. "And I imagine you will find some of the comfort you need amongst a room of fellow survivors."

For the first time, the concept struck me that my narrow, isolated island might not be as secluded as I'd always assumed. I guess I knew at a high level there were others, of course, but not until now did I let it resonate that I may be part of something bigger than myself. And that I might be able to say these dark, horrible things out loud and have someone else nod knowingly and just calmly say, "that happened to me, too." The idea was terrifying and exhilarating, and I couldn't seem to settle on a middle ground.

"We're almost out of time for today, but I'll get you the information for this support group, and I'd like you to make a commitment to at least go a couple times and try it out. Okay?"

I nodded.

"Great. And I'm going to call the student health center to set up your bi-weekly therapy sessions. If you want to sign this release form, I can fax it to them, and that would enable me to check-in and get updates from your therapist at school. That way, if you're home for the summer or want to see me again at any time, I'll be up to speed on your care."

I nodded again.

"But, Andrea, if the report comes back that you're not going and you don't keep your commitment to your mental health care, I would like your permission to discuss that with your parents. Nothing specific about our conversations or anything like that, of course, just about the frequency and consistency of your appointments to ensure you're staying on top of it."

"Yeah. Okay," I said, with a mix of defeat and relief.

As I left her office and headed to my car in the chilly parking lot, I tucked the slip of paper with the support group details safely into my wallet and let myself fall into the driver's seat in a huff of exhaustion. I wanted to unwrap the past hour and analyze what had just happened, but it was too big to swallow in one bite.

As I started the car and backed out of the parking space, hearing the freshly fallen snow crunch against the heavy tires, my body begged to just go home and lie down so I could rest and process. But there was one more stop I needed to make first.

I turned my car off when I arrived outside the sprawling single-level home with blue shutters, tucked neatly behind a quiet golf course. I sank down in my seat and pulled the faux fur hood of my winter coat tightly around my face, so only my eyes peered out from the driver's side window.

As I studied the pristine outside of Josh's house, I wondered if he was home. I wondered if he'd sent me that e-mail from his basement bedroom, sitting atop those starchy flannel sheets and musty checkered comforter. Or maybe he was somewhere else entirely, a different state or country even, going to new restaurants and meeting new people who had no idea they'd just had a brush with evil. Or maybe he'd changed, for real this time, and had a new girlfriend he treated nicely and wrote poetry about. I hated all of these options. Any form of the present that didn't involve him feeling cold, desperate, and alone, preferably filled with agony and regret, just didn't seem good enough. But since I didn't know the truth, it gave me temporary solace to pretend he was miserable, even though deep down, we both knew he'd gotten away with all of it.

There didn't appear to be any movement in the house. There were no cars in the driveway, and the curtains were all drawn. The house just stood there, polished and sturdy, unaware of the horror it had sheltered for so long. And at that moment, I wondered what it would be like if I could see this house as what it was ... just a house; just a pile of wood and bricks and tile with a half-circle paved driveway and a manicured lawn.

I didn't even realize I was crying until I heard the choking sobs rush from my throat into the frozen air of my old Pontiac. I expelled the panic that would swell in my chest every time I drove by this hateful house, angry at its outer suburban flair that did nothing to warn passerby of the darkness that swallowed those who entered and spit them out to never be the same.

I forced out the memory of our first kiss on that crisp autumn afternoon in his room, where I buzzed with anticipation and floated away in the high you can only get from sparkly teenage lust. And I purged the dreams he shattered each day after that from his purposeful, torturous blows that burrowed under my skin and made my bones ache. There was a release with each sob, and with each release, there was a crumb that led me closer to daylight.

It felt good to cry. It felt good to scream. My lungs burned with the newfound realization of being alive as the house started to look more like a house. Just a place that some sad, angry people lived in, unsure of how to express the pain that came with walking on broken glass for years at a time.

I wiped my face with my coat sleeve as my breathing steadied from desperate gulps to deep exhales. I wasn't sure what was different now, but something was. And I was ready to drive away from this place for the last time.

As I started the car, my mind flashed to every other time I'd pulled away from this house, often holding my tears back until I turned onto the main road. I would make the short drive from his house to mine, collect myself, and straighten the mask I needed to re-enter the public, telling myself I wouldn't keep going back there. But the next day, I'd find myself there again, as if pulled by a force I couldn't break. And the more I tried, the deeper I fell, so I eventually stopped trying.

I was ready to go home now, but first, I picked up my phone and opened the Josh e-mail. Before I could re-read it, I closed my eyes and pressed "delete." And then it was gone. Just like that, it was gone. Something resembling joy came out of my body in a burst of laughter I could barely contain. It was like that tap of my finger had shifted the Earth, and I was suddenly rife with energy.

I started driving away, the house disappearing from my rearview mirror. And every inch that created space between me and that place felt sacred.

I pulled over into a nearby shopping center parking lot with a delirious exhilaration pulsing through me. And in my shameless, unabashed fog, I picked up my phone to make a call.

Chapter Nineteen

"Hello?" Carter's clear, lucid voice washed over me from the other end of my phone.

"Carter! Hi! It's Andie!" I echoed joyously. "It's so good to hear your voice."

"Yeah. Hi, Andie. Everything okay?" he asked quietly and directly.

"Yes! Great, actually."

"Good. That's good."

"I'm in Oakwood right now, and I just... I've had a crazy day. I'm feeling a lot of things, and I just needed you to know that I think I'm really, like, getting better, you know? I feel like I have my head on straight for the first time in a long time," I said quickly, my words pouring over the top of each other to get out.

"Well, I'm happy for you," he replied. "Did you need something?"

"It's just been a long time since we talked. Not since, well, you know. And I've been thinking a lot, and I'm ready to make some big changes. I don't want to be the same girl you had to take care of and worry about. I'm ready. I'm ready to be with you in this whole new way, the way that you deserve."

I held my breath, shaken by my own vulnerability, and waited anxiously for his response.

"Hello? Are you there?" I squeaked through a long, painful pause, my mind racing to visualize him in this moment, wondering where he was and what he was wearing, and how his face looked as he heard my pleas. I pictured him in his dimly lit bedroom, in the middle of some kind of modern, artsy drawing, when his eyes lit up as my name popped onto his phone.

"Andrea..." he started, as though unsure of how

to finish his thought. "I'm with Olivia now."

"Yeah, well, you were with Sloane when we first got together, so…"

No response. I continued.

"Carter, you know, you never called or texted after I moved. Not to check in or see if I was okay or ask how Chicago is or anything. How come?" I blurted, realizing with each ungraceful word that this was the first time I was willing to consider an actual answer to this question.

"I've been really busy."

"Okay, but nobody is too busy to send a text." I laughed. "Did you just … not want to talk to me?"

The silence from his side began to bury me.

"Never mind, it's fine. I'm here now," I replied, trying to shake off the sirens ringing loudly from inside my body. "And honestly, I understand why it didn't work out with us before. I know I was a mess, but I'm getting my shit together. And, and we're meant to be together. I … I need you."

"I'm sorry, Andie. Take care of yourself, okay?"

"Carter! No, no … this is *not* how this ends for us." My chin began to tremble as I processed his words through a quickly collapsing stupor.

The phone clicked as he ended the call, and I sat frozen in my car as people milled by in the crowded parking lot.

I'd always thought that if things ended with Carter and me, it'd be burned down in the brightest fire, with the same intense flame that started it. We'd part ways with singed skin and charred lungs, grateful for every gasp of clean air we took before the fire consumed us. But instead, it flickered out, slowly and all at once, where I sat begging him to love me and him quickly and brilliantly forgetting he ever had.

Before I could fully react, I instinctively went to text Ethan for help and comfort, but I retracted my hand as if I'd touched an electric bolt when I remembered what I had done. My heart sank and spiraled as I realized angrily that my most cherished relationships were being picked off one by one and that I was alone behind the trigger.

I called Stephanie instead. She had always been the last house on the block for me, and I felt sick with guilt that I'd managed to turn something beautiful that had resulted in cute knitted friendship bracelets into a one-sided pity party that she had to constantly carry me out of.

"Hey, Andie, what's up?" she chirped on the other line. The pep and kindness in her voice made me feel even worse, but true to form, I unloaded about my conversation with Carter.

"So, what should I do now?" I asked when I finished the story. "Should I give him some time to come around and call again in a few days? Or maybe write him a letter?"

"No, hon," Stephanie replied plainly. "It's over. It was over months ago. The world doesn't change just because you do."

"But ... but ... but I really love him," I stammered, wiping hot tears from my flushed face. "I need him, Steph. He's the love of my life."

"No, he is just a very pretty distraction that made you feel special for a little while. Remember, he is not the stars, the moon, and the sky all wrapped into one, Andie. You are."

"Then why do I ruin everything?" I shouted.

"Did you ever even ask Carter if he wanted to move?" she asked pointedly.

"Of course I did," I snapped.

"Yeah? When?"

I paused and thought. "Well, we just *knew* we were going to be together, and I decided to go to Columbia, so it just, it just made sense."

"Okay. Another question. Why didn't Ethan come over last night? Normally he would've thrown himself into traffic to get to your house when you needed him."

"It's a long story," I lied.

"I bet."

"Why are you doing this?" I begged.

"I'm not doing anything. I love you, Andie. God knows one of us has to. But you need to know that other people don't change just because we're ready. I think probably you didn't have the healthiest thing with Carter. Someone can only be hero worshiped for so long before it starts to get old. And yeah, I think it's too late, no matter how much you're ready to change. And I think you probably fucked up with Ethan, too. And I don't know if that one is fixable or what, but sometimes when we hurt people, we just need to sit with that for a minute. Some things are permanent, but we move on anyway, even when it really, really sucks. Maybe it's time to focus on yourself for a little bit? I think we all miss that pink-haired emo girl." She laughed. "And honestly, I don't know who told you that blondes have more fun, but…"

"Shut up," I said playfully through my tears.

"You're going to be okay, hon. I promise."

"Steph, I'm really lucky to have you in my life. I'm sorry I don't say that more often. And I'm sorry I've barely asked you how you're doing. I just feel so … confused?" I couldn't find the words as I began to crash from the jittery high that launched me from Josh's house to this parking lot in a whoosh of sudden self-righteousness.

"One day at a time," she replied softly. "You just need to take this all one day at a time. That's all any of us can really do."

I smiled through my tear-stained face. "I'm a mess," I admitted through a partial laugh.

"We're all kinda a mess. You're in good company."

"Thank you, Stephanie. I love you."

"I love you, too, but listen, I know it's not your fault that these things happened to you, but at a certain point, Andie, it *is* your fault that you've refused to get help. So if you're not willing to just *try* now, then I don't know if I can keep making up for your part of this friendship. I want to be here for you, but I also need to set my own boundaries."

"I understand," I said honestly, wiping the tears from my face. "And I don't know how exactly yet, but I know I *want* to feel better. God, I really want to feel better. And clearly, my way isn't working." I laughed.

"Ya think?" she teased.

Chapter Twenty

"Are you sure you're okay?" my mom asked at the train station as I prepared to head back to Chicago.

"No, I'm not. But ... I think I'm ready to be okay," I replied.

"Check in every day, at least a text," she reminded me as she hugged me tightly.

"I promise," I said, relieved at how the truth sounded in my voice. "Thanks, Mom. I love you."

"I love you more." She smiled.

As I settled into my seat on the train, I saw her out the window, waving eagerly and blowing kisses. I rolled my eyes and laughed, blowing her a final kiss as a grin swept over my weary face.

When the train started moving, and it became clear the seat beside me was empty, I kicked my feet up and pulled out my leopard-print notebook.

WHAT I WANT I scrawled in big, bold letters at the top of the page. Dr. Hawthorne had always said that the best way to find out who I am is to start by understanding what I want, and then everything in between will fill itself out.

I sat pensive, staring at the page, unsure of where or how to start this time. Thinking of what I wrote before I left for college made me feel sick and sad and desperate for a rewrite.

When I was with Josh, I'd never thought about the future. It was all I had to just survive each day, each hour, each minute, that any thought of future hopes and dreams would've been an indulgent luxury I couldn't afford. And then, being with Carter, my future just felt so clear because he *was* my future. I would've followed that man to the ends of the Earth if he had let me. So I'd never thought about what I wanted from *my* life since having him felt like having everything already. But now here I was, alone, with permission to dream but left in starless insomnia. So I took a deep breath and tried to quiet my mind and let my hand jot down whatever needed to flow out.

I want to be a journalist. An award-winning investigative journalist that uncovers truths and changes minds. I want to graduate from college. Find real love. And start a family. I smiled as I wrote that, but couldn't ignore the nagging clutch on my heart that told me Carter *was* my one chance at real love, and I blew it by being with him when I wasn't ready. As I tried to shake off the thought, the guilt crept back in as my mind wandered to Ethan. I opened my phone and sent him a text.

Me: **I'm sorry. Can we talk?**

I set the phone down as I wrote and watched the landscape rush by me outside the cold, wide window. I turned my ringer up high so I'd be sure to hear if he replied. He didn't.

I stopped writing my list. Maybe I'd skipped too many steps before I was ready to feel dreamy and hopeful. Maybe Stephanie was right, and I needed to let myself sit in the pain for a while first. But this time, on the train ride from Oakwood to Chicago, I didn't bury anything on the suburban Illinois outskirts along the way. I wore it all and let it burn. I hated it, but at least it was mine.

****

I edged the door to my dorm room open quietly as I nervously awaited Hannah's reaction to my awkward disappearing act.

"Han?" I called out through the dusky, open room. When I realized she wasn't home, I kicked my shoes off and flopped down at my desk, sighing as I opened my laptop, preparing for a flood of missed assignments and shared study notes I didn't feel like facing yet. When my phone dinged, I grabbed the welcome distraction but let out a disappointed grunt when I saw Dean's name.

Dean: **Come over tonight?**

I started to type back a polite decline, the first one I would've ever given him, but I paused as I thought about how soothing it might be to feel someone's hands against my skin. I started to get lost in the cloudy thoughts as my mind pictured the warmth of a body that grabbed at me in purposeful lust, and I felt a shiver at the base of my spine.

Maybe I would go over tonight and take my mind off of the leftover humiliation that beckoned to be unearthed after my conversation with Carter. Perhaps I could stave it off a day if I let myself get lost in the high of feeling desired. But I couldn't get Stephanie's words out of my head. And I wondered if the girl who felt powerful as she drove far away from Josh's house would approve of this persistent art of numbing. But that girl also drove straight from that nightmare into a crumbled fantasy, so maybe I shouldn't trust her quite yet.

Me: **I can't tonight.**

I sent the text before I could talk myself back into it. I waited for a response where he begged me to reconsider, giving me some crumb of feeling to last me a little while, but it never came. He probably just scrolled to the next girl in his contact list and pasted the same text until he got a yes. I bet it didn't take long.

I closed my laptop and grabbed the plastic shopping bag I'd gotten at the drug store on my way back from Union Station. Lugging it with me to the community dorm bathroom in the hallway, I pulled out the hot pink hair dye and plopped it on the sink counter in front of me. A smile formed on my face so wide that my cheeks ached. I bit my lip, tapped my fingers, and ripped the box open eagerly, feeling giddy as the contents fell out onto the counter.

It came back to me like muscle memory as I adorned the plastic gloves that felt like tissue paper and mixed the magenta dye with the little plastic paintbrush that came with the kit. A few girls walked in and out as I painted, starting with my roots, but nobody commented. It certainly wasn't the weirdest thing they'd seen in this bathroom.

I hummed as I painted, stretching each piece of hair to saturate every section until I was covered from scalp to tip. I looked in the mirror and laughed when I saw the messy pink glob of hair that was piled wet atop my head as the dye processed. I snapped a selfie and sent it to Stephanie. The champagne highlights were gone, and my face was clean from the heavy powders and lashes I'd become so accustomed to wearing all day and night.

"Cav?" Hannah's voice rang out behind me as the bathroom door swung open.

"Oh, hey!" I shouted gleefully.

"You're back? What are you doing to your hair?" She gasped.

"Dying it pink, like how I used to have it. You like it?"

"Umm, it's a bit … pink?" she said, eyes wide.

"Haha, that's the point!" I laughed.

"You seem … happy?" she guessed. "Are you okay? Are you back for good? I was worried. I know you texted me that you went home for a bit, but I don't know. I was worried. You barely responded to me while you were gone."

"I'm good!" I said. "Or, I'm at least trying to get

there. It's been a weird few days."

"I can see that," she said as she studied my hair. "Is it gonna look *that* pink?" She pointed to the picture on the box.

"I hope so!"

"It would seem I still have a lot to learn about you, Cav." She laughed.

"Andie," I replied. "You can call me Andie."

"Okay, *Andie*, it would seem like I still have a lot to learn about you, *Andie*. I like it."

At that moment, my phone buzzed, and I looked down.

"Oh, shit, it's already five?" I asked.

"Yeah, I was just gonna grab a shower and go to the library for a while before going out later. What about you?"

"I, uh, I have a thing to go to in an hour," I stammered, hiding the reminder on my phone that displayed the support group address. "And I need to wash this dye out so we can see my masterpiece."

"Yeah, okay, well hey, I'm glad you're back. Let's catch up later," she said as she put her shower caddy in an open stall, swiping the heavy plastic curtain behind her as she began to undress behind it.

"Actually..." I mused, suddenly gaining some confidence now that she was out of sight. "Maybe you want to come with me? It's in walking distance and starts at six."

"What is it?" she asked as I heard the shower turn on. "I hate how long this water takes to warm up." She groaned as her workout bra and t-shirt flung over the shower rod to hang against the curtain.

"It's a support group. For survivors of domestic violence and sexual assault."

The shower curtain zipped open forcefully as she

stuck her head out. "Shh!" she whispered aggressively. "Are you insane?"

"Well, I'm gonna go. Just to check it out. And I thought maybe you…"

"Keep your voice down! Jesus, Cav."

"Andie," I reminded her.

"Whatever," she snapped as she pulled the curtain shut again.

"Okay, well, if you change your mind—"

"Yep! Talk later!" she yelled as I shrugged.

The world doesn't change because we're ready, I reminded myself as Stephanie's voice rang in my ears. I wouldn't force Hannah to be ready. I wasn't even sure if I was ready. I just knew that what I was doing wasn't working.

I got into the shower stall next to Hannah's to wash out my hair dye and beamed as I saw the water run hot pink streams over my body and trickle down the drain. By the time I got out, Hannah was gone. I quickly dried off and wrapped the towel around my body before slipping back out to the mirror and turning on my hairdryer. I swept the hot air through my damp hair and brushed it as I dried. It wasn't perfect; since I'd had highlights before, it made for an uneven blend, leaving some sections a darker fuchsia shade and others lighter like a strawberry lollipop. I couldn't have loved it more. I squealed and clasped my hands together when I saw the finished product. There I was, familiar and imperfect, with bags under my eyes and hair like bubblegum. And it felt exactly right.

Chapter Twenty-One

I felt my freshly dyed hair bounce around me as I walked briskly on the frosted sidewalk toward the YWCA. I kept my head down in hopes nobody would recognize me as I got closer, pushing the lobby door open with my shoulder as I kicked the snow off my boots in the entryway. I checked my phone. It was 5:58. I looked around the lobby for signs to point me in the right direction. I hated being late.

There were two long hallways that had several identical doors with numbers on top. I had no idea what room the group was in.

"Do you need help?" an older Black woman with short grey hair and a warm smile asked from behind the front desk.

"No," I barked quickly. "Sorry, I mean, I don't know."

"Okay, well, I'm happy to help. What are you looking for?"

"I don't know," I said dizzily as my breath quickened. "Never mind, this was a mistake." I turned toward the front door. Maybe I wasn't ready yet. Maybe I never would be.

"The survivors' group meets in room three-B, just down that hall to the left," she said gently.

"How did..." I trailed off as I stared through her.

"It's okay. Everyone has a first day. You're safe here, honey." She stood up to point me toward the right hallway.

I felt a lump form in my throat at the concept of being safe anywhere. I opened my mouth to thank her, but couldn't speak without releasing the tears that were holding firm behind my eyelids, so I just stumbled toward room three-B.

I closed my eyes, took a breath, and opened the door a crack. Peering in, I saw a circle of rusty folding chairs in a comfortable room filled with motivational posters, a big bookshelf overflowing with self-help literature, and an array of other donated furniture, throw pillows, and file cabinets. There were at least twenty women in the circle, maybe more, with only a few empty chairs. I quietly scooted the door open just enough to slip in and scurried to the first empty chair I saw, sitting down without making eye contact with anyone.

"Did you see the coffee machine finally works?" said the curvy redhead next to me as she motioned to the table by the door that held an old silver appliance and a tray of mismatched mugs. I shook my head, looking up at her.

"Sarah?" I asked, immediately recognizing my work frenemy from Blush.

"Andrea? I didn't recognize you with the hair…"

"Yeah, it's new. Sorry, I … I didn't know you came here. This is my first time."

"Hey, it's okay." Her eyes softened as she looked at me. "I'm happy you're here. And this is all confidential, okay? So just … at work and stuff…"

"Of course," I said, motioning to zip my lips. "Not a word."

"Thanks. And after, let me know if you have any questions. This group saved my life. I've been coming here for years."

"Wow," I said breathlessly. "I had no idea."

She smiled meekly. "I guess you never really know what someone else is going through."

"Okay, ladies, let's get started," a welcoming voice rang from the other side of the circle. "I'm Kim, your group leader. Welcome."

As Kim spoke, my mind wandered, and I started looking around the room. I gasped silently when I recognized Rachel, the perky brunette from the front row of my communications class. She caught my eye and looked away quickly. Next to her was Vanessa, who lived down the hall from me. A few chairs over was Lacey, the graduate assistant from my journalism class, and down the row from her was Kat, the barista from the coffee shop by my dorm who always made my double espressos and laughed when I'd quickly chase it with swigs of diet soda. And then I saw Hannah Taylor. Looking at the floor and tapping her heel impatiently on the tile.

She came! I thought as my heart swelled to see her. I wanted to pause time and hug her for being here to support me.

"Hannah, do you want to get us started with sharing?" Kim asked. Hannah shook her head. "Okay, Tiffany, how about you?"

It was not Hannah's first time at the group. The realization washed over me as I exhaled the shock. She was not here to support me. She was here because she needed to be. Just like I did. Just like Sarah did. Just like Rachel, Vanessa, Lacey, and Kat. I had never been alone. Despite my shameful and deafening assumptions that I was the only person broken enough to feel this way, I'd been surrounded by others who were hiding in plain sight.

Sarah kicked me from under our chairs to pull me back into the moment.

"Huh?" I asked, confused.

"I was just asking if this was your first time?" Kim was looking at me.

"Sorry, um, yes, it is," I said. Hannah finally looked at me, a tear streaming from her eye, her face soft and somber. She gave me a knowing smile.

"I'm sorry," she mouthed from across the circle. I placed my hand over my heart to show her I wasn't mad. She was allowed to have secrets, too.

"Welcome home," Kim said. "What's your first name?"

"Andrea. Or Andie," I replied softly.

"Do you want to share with the group what brought you here today?"

I looked around the room at the other women. They were all of different ages, sizes, and colors. They, too, had shown up on a dark wintry evening to fight their demons through a secret sisterhood I never knew existed. Hannah wiped the tear from her face and made heavy eye contact with me. She nodded in encouragement, and I felt a new, clean breath of air fill my lungs for the first time.

"Yes," I said, feeling the strength of the room lift my voice. "I'm ready."

The End

Evernight Teen ®

www.evernightteen.com

CPSIA information can be obtained
at www.ICGtesting.com
Printed in the USA
LVHW051653240521
688348LV00005B/156